Praise For

Zebedee's Calling

A rare, historically accurate fictional epic that is an inspiration for today's youth, *Zebedee's Calling* represents Joel's unique approach to story-telling and stimulates both introspection and action: What is the place of the Bible in today's society? What is our obligation to ensure people have access to the Holy Scriptures? And most importantly, what can the coming generation do to re-ignite our passion for God, for country, and for the salvation of the world?
—Andrew Friedel, *President, Christian Fellowship Church of Kitchener-Waterloo*

***

Joel encapsulates the essence of "true" Christianity in *Zebedee's Calling*. Although the characters may be fictitious, the storyline is very relatable through the ages. I was particularly impressed with his use of thought processes when one is questioning true believers on God's existence and Zebedee's responses which unequivocally removed any doubt. I thoroughly enjoyed the glimpse into the interesting historical culture, with associated terminology and the evolution through the passage of time. My key take-away is that Salvation comes not from religion, but from our relationship with God. A real gem for believers and non-believers, young and old!
—Sharen Way, *Ontario, Canada*

***

Joel Francis has written an exciting, action-filled story of a young hero, Zebedee, whose courage and loyalty are challenged in the face of danger. Decision-making, family values, trustworthy friendships, and a growing faith are blended together to make this historically-based story a must read for any young reader.

—Pastor Paul G. Knauer, *BS, BEd, MA in Christian School Administration, MDiv.*

ZEBEDEE'S CALLING

A Hero's Quest for the Word

Joel Francis

TABLE OF CONTENTS

Introduction

Even as Christianity spread rapidly in the Roman Empire and other parts of the world during the 1st Century AD, paganism and other false teachings were creeping into the Church. These attacks from the enemy did not go unnoticed by the writers of the New Testament.

The most notable among the heresies was praying to saints and praying for the dead, which became widespread in the 4th Century.[1] Sacraments performed under the authority of the church began to be viewed as rituals necessary for salvation by an increasing number of Christians. In the absence of copies of the Scriptures in the hands of the common man, the clergy enforced good works as determined by their own whim and fancy as additional requirements for piety and eternal life. There have been many who opposed these false teachings that were prevalent in their time. This is evident from studying the history of the Roman churches through the centuries.

It is customary to think that before October 31, 1517, when Martin Luther posted his famous Ninety-five Theses on the door of a church in Wittenberg, all Christians belonged to either the Western Roman Church, which is now called the Roman Catholic Church, or the Eastern Roman Church, which is now called the Eastern Orthodox Church. That notion is far from the truth.

However, there have always been Christians who knew that the Lord Jesus Christ Himself, not the bishop of Rome, nor the archbishop of Constantinople, is the Head of the Church. Additionally, there were also reformers inside the Roman Catholic Church before Martin Luther posted his Ninety-five Theses. There was Peter Waldo, who was born in the 12th Century, and John Wycliffe and Jan Hus, both of whom were born in the 14th Century. The reformers agreed many of their beliefs differed from the teaching of the Roman Catholic Church. One of their tenets was that the Holy Bible was the only authority on matters of faith and the Christian life.

Two notable "proto-Protestants," i.e., Protestants before the year 1517, who lived in the 4th and 5th Centuries were a monk named Jovinian and a presbyter named Vigilantus[2]. There was also a proto-Protestant in the 9th Century named Claudius[3], who was the bishop of Turin from the years 817 to 827. These three publicly disagreed with some of the teachings of the Church of Rome. But has the reader heard the tale of the Bible believing Christians and forerunners of Anabaptists, in England, in the 11th Century? If not, you are in for an interesting ride.

In those days, England was called Engla Land and English was called Englisċ. Those names are used throughout this story. Also in the story the name "Jacobus" is used instead of the more modern form "James" because the form "James" was introduced to England in a later century and comes from the French form of the same name.

Bede, an 8th century Anglo-Saxon monk and historian writes about St. Augustine, who was sent by King Æthelberht and Pope Gregory to Engla Land as a missionary to the pagan Anglo-Saxons in the late 6th century.[4]

By the end of the 7th Century, Christianity as a religion was well-established in England. The religious practices mostly consisted of the sacraments of the Western Roman Church at the time, as well as giving gifts to churches and monasteries and alms to the poor as acts of "penance". Church leaders made themselves intermediaries between the laity and God[5]. Teachings on faith in God and a relationship with God as vividly described in the Old Testament and passionately followed in the New Testament were not common.

Both formal and anonymous copies of translations of the Bible existed in various languages by the timeframe of this story[6], but the Western Roman Church held their services in Latin, which only thegns could understand to some extent; the services in the Eastern Roman Church were conducted in Greek.

Coming to the story, it will be important for the reader to remember the social structure of the time. The upper class Anglo-Saxons, who were called thegns, could afford to send their children to monasteries to study. The lower class, who were called ceorls, could not afford this luxury. Many thegns owned slaves, who were called thralls.

CHAPTER 1

SIMON AND PRISCILLA'S FAMILY

This story begins in London, Engla Land in 1041 AD. The Bible had not yet been divided into chapters and verses. The calendar of Julius Caesar from 46 BC was still in common use and would remain so in most of Western Europe until 1582. Although France had a king, many of the dukes were too powerful for the king to control, so they did as they pleased.

Harthacnut, king of Engla Land and of Denmark, on the other hand, enjoyed the loyalty of his subjects, including the eorls in Engla Land and the jarls in Denmark. Both eorls and jarls were men of nobility who served their kings. Huscarls were thegns who were elite, fulltime soldiers serving as a ruler's personal army.

"Priscilla, I have great news," Simon exclaimed to the woman he loved.

"What is it, Simon?" asked Priscilla.

"We won't have to sell ourselves into bondage once we get married," said Simon. "The king has agreed to let me become one of his huscarls."

Simon and Priscilla were two lovers born into wealthy families of thegns, which were of the upper class but not the nobility. Their families hated each other and their parents strictly forbade them from marrying each other. They eloped and, as a result, their parents disinherited them, as they had warned them they would.

Simon was a strong man, so he entered the service of Harthacnut, king of Engla Land, as a huscarl to support himself and Priscilla.

The next year King Harthacnut died during a wedding because he drank too much alcohol. His half-brother, Edward, succeeded him as the king of Engla Land, since the unmarried Harthacnut was childless. Simon continued serving as a huscarl under King Edward, even though most huscarls left the royal service and sought employment with the eorls instead. Many of them joined the personal service of Godwin, earl of Wessex.

Simon and Priscilla missed their parents and siblings but did not regret running away. That same year, Priscilla gave birth to their first child, a boy. They named him John. Two years later she bore another child, also a boy. They named their second son Jacobus. Their third child, a girl, lived only a few days. Then, on Wednesday, April 5, 1049, Priscilla gave birth to their fourth child.

"It's a boy," the midwife told Priscilla, as the child let out a vociferous first cry.

Simon made no delay in getting him baptized that very day, in case he died a few days after birth like his sister had. His parents did not want him to be thrown in hell or limbo. Although there was still a debate in the Church of Rome about what happened to unbaptized babies who died, Simon and Priscilla wanted all their sons to be received into Heaven and enjoy being in the presence of the Lord forever.[7]

Priscilla, still recovering from childbirth, could not attend the baptism ceremony.

"Have you decided on a name?" the priest asked Simon, ritualistically.

"Yes," replied Simon. "His name is Zebedee."

"What?" asked the priest confused, but rather amused.

"Is there a problem?" Simon queried, visibly irritated, although just slightly.

"No," responded the priest, clearing his throat.

"I baptize you Zebedee, son of Simon and Priscilla, in the Name of the Father, and of the Son, and of the Holy Spirit," announced the priest, while baptizing the infant.

After the ceremony the priest took Simon aside to talk privately.

"So, why did you choose the name Zebedee?" he asked Simon.

"It is the name of one of my great-granduncles," Simon lied, a little annoyed.

"Oh," the priest replied.

"Why do you ask?" questioned Simon.

"Well," he began, "his older brothers' names are John and Jacobus."

"So what?" asked Simon.

"As you know, our Lord had two disciples named Jacobus, and one of them had a brother named John," he continued to elucidate his knowledge of the Scriptures to the member of his parish, who was obviously ignorant of who Zebedee was in the Bible.

"Yes, I know this," Simon responded.

"John and Jacobus had a father..." he went on.

Simon looked at the old man with a little more irritation, wishing he would not probe so much, but then calmed himself.

"...whose name was Zebedee."

"Oh," exclaimed Simon, surprised. "His godparents didn't tell me or Priscilla this when we told them what we were planning to name him, but why does it matter?"

"I guess it doesn't matter," the priest said and then sighed. "But it is not a common name, how did you hear of it?"

"It was John's suggestion and we liked it," Simon admitted. "He said it is a name in the Gospels and that a priest told him about it."

Then the two men noticed young John laughing.

"Why are you laughing, son?" Simon asked, amused.

"I asked a priest if Jacobus and John's father's name was mentioned in the Bible because I thought it would be funny if our youngest brother was given that name," John replied, putting his hand on Jacobus' shoulder.

Upon hearing this, young Jacobus began to giggle. This made the two men laugh as well, until the priest quickly composed himself and said, "I have another baptism to attend to."

Most thegns sent their children to monasteries to study religion, philosophy, literature, history, writing, and arithmetic for a few years. While Zebedee was an average student, Latin was his favorite subject, although he did not achieve fluency by the end of his education. Jacobus and John were always at the tops of their classes. The ardent desire for further education and the lack of desire to lead a conjugal life were contributors to John requesting the permission of his father to study an additional year. Simon reluctantly agreed.

John always felt called to know God better and to dedicate his life to his Creator. At the age of fifteen, much to the disappointment of his father, John left his parents' house to live in a monastery and made his vows of poverty, chastity, and obedience.[8]

In the year 1058, Simon and Priscilla's relatives reconciled with each other and with them. Both sets of parents died in the following eight years, leaving an equal inheritance for all their children. After their deaths, upon Priscilla's entreating, Simon asked King Edward if he could retire from being a huscarl. King Edward granted his request.

King Edward died without children soon after that on January 5, 1066, but not before choosing Harold, son of Godwin, as his successor. Harold had led Engla Land's armies into battle and was considered to be the second most powerful man in Engla Land before he became the king of Engla Land.

At this point in time, Simon and Priscilla owned fifteen hides of farm land in a village adjacent to London. A hide was a tract of land sufficient to support a family. Hide-holdings were the basis of taxation. Simon's and Priscilla's holding was a wheat farm on which thirty ceorls, or free peasants, were employed to work.

Simon and Priscilla also had two slaves, twins named Hilda and Leofric. One of Hilda and Leofric's forefathers had been captured in battle and enslaved, therefore, all his descendants had become slaves as well.

On the morning of Tuesday, September 19, 1066, Jacobus and Zebedee were sparring with wooden seaxes. A seax was either a single-edged knife or short, single-edged sword; the former was used as a tool and the latter was used as a weapon. Only long, double-edged swords were called swords. Wooden weapons were made for practice and were a little lighter than their metal counterparts. Every Anglo-Saxon man, and some women, always carried a seax with them, and those who owned a sword always carried it with them as well.

Jacobus had to be ready for battle at any moment. King Harold Godwinson had been anticipating an invasion from William, duke of Normandy, a dukedom in northern France, but he had to send his army back home to harvest earlier that month, as supplies were running thin. However, everyone knew that an invasion was imminent.

Jacobus and Zebedee had practiced with long wooden spears and shields the day before. The spear was a thegn's primary weapon. Jacobus used a seax as his secondary weapon. They used real shields while sparring; shields were wooden so there were no practice shields.

Simon was busy at home, and Samson, a ceorl, or freeman, who worked for him, was already working in the field. So Jacobus couldn't practice with either of them that day. Both Simon and Samson were trained and experienced warriors, as they had been huscarls. They were also renowned for their gallantry. Simon was a war hero because he had saved King Harold's life in battle in the past. Samson was a war hero too, because he killed more enemies in battle than any other Anglo-Saxon alive.

Jacobus and Zebedee were supposed to help with the harvesting since their parents couldn't afford to hire more workers, but they decided to practice fighting for a bit before they went to their parents' farm. So here they were behind their parents' rectangular, wooden, thatched roof house. The house was twenty-one feet wide and thirty-three feet long. An Anglo-Saxon foot was thirteen and two-tenths inches of today's measurements.

Their parents would not let Zebedee become a warrior. They thought he was not quite strong enough because he was slightly weaker than an average man and they only needed to supply the king with three warriors, one for every five hides of land they possessed. Regardless, Zebedee enjoyed combat training, so Jacobus and Zebedee sometimes trained together.

Jacobus was battle ready when he was fifteen, which was the minimum age to be recruited into the army. Simon and Priscilla paid Samson to be the third warrior they needed to supply the king. They had been doing so for years. Samson, like most ceorls, did not have any land of his own at this point of time.

Most huscarls did not own land, but Samson had been rewarded with some land because of his battle feats. However, he had to relinquish his land when he left the king's service.

For the first time, both Jacobus and Zebedee disarmed each other at the same time.

"It's a draw," Zebedee exclaimed joyfully.

Jacobus always won. Zebedee was exhilarated, but just as the word "draw" came out of his mouth, Jacobus tackled him to the ground, got up, and made punching motions towards his face. Jacobus then grabbed his seax, giving Zebedee enough time to get up, and then he made slashing motions at Zebedee with it.

"I suppose it's not a draw then," Zebedee said and let out a sigh.

"You have to be ready for anything on the battlefield," Jacobus told his little brother. "If both you and your enemy are disarmed, use your hand-to-hand fighting skills. If your enemy is armed while you are disarmed, then you need to run and pick up a weapon as soon as you can before you engage them in battle. You haven't defeated your enemy unless you kill them or they surrender."

"Oh, all right," Zebedee sighed. "I will remember that if I ever fight in a battle."

"Oh, I forgot." Jacobus replied. "Sorry."

"It's nothing I can change," Zebedee answered, wearing a mock smile.

"I suppose I just wanted to teach someone what our father and Samson taught me about fighting," Jacobus explained. "And I need to practice, too. By the way, you are improving very quickly."

"My disarming you was probably just a fluke," Zebedee responded and feigned a laugh.

Suddenly Priscilla yelled from behind Zebedee, "Stop wasting time! Make yourselves useful and go buy some eggs, fish, fruits, and vegetables, since you aren't harvesting like you should be."

Jacobus and Zebedee turned to see their mother standing at a corner of the house with a stern expression. There were two big straw baskets full of wheat beside her.

"You can use this wheat to trade," she continued. "We need peas, carrots, turnips, apples, and any other fruit of your choice."

Once they had the baskets securely on their backs, she handed Zebedee a silver penny.

"This is one of the pennies we received for selling the deer your father hunted last month," she told Zebedee and Jacobus. "Use it only if you need to."

As they were on their way to the market, Zebedee realized that Jacobus had let him disarm him of his weapon on purpose, so he could teach him hand-to-hand combat, as well as help Zebedee's confidence. *Perhaps he wanted to teach me to defend myself just in case I ever need to*, Zebedee thought.

When they had nearly reached the marketplace, Zebedee saw a group of young men he once thought were his friends till they began to make fun of him. As he walked past them, he recalled them saying things like, "Look, it is a feather light thegn," or "Why are you so short and skinny?" or "Is that a walking, talking skeleton?" or "What a loser?"

Then Zebedee's thoughts took him to an incident a year ago, when they were making fun of him, and he had summarized a couple of passages from Scripture that John had told him about.

"God works all things together for the good of those who love Him. We are more than conquerors through Jesus!" was Zebedee's reply that day. "You tell me, how can someone who is more than a conqueror be a loser?"

"What? What is that?" one of them asked.

"I think it is some kind of a proverb," another quipped.

"Where did you get that from?" a third asked.

"That is what the Scripture tells us," Zebedee told them. "In the Book of Romans."

"How do you know what's in the Scriptures?" one of them asked angrily.

"John told me," Zebedee replied.

John by then had studied the Bible quite enthusiastically at the monastery. He would often teach verses to his family members whenever he met them.

After that day they didn't dare make fun of Zebedee again. They were Christians, after all, and they did have some fear of God, even though they were not very religious. Zebedee's family was very religious, they trusted God and sought to obey Him with great conviction.

"What do we need to buy again?" Jacobus' question brought Zebedee back to the present.

Before Zebedee could answer his question, the voices from the marketplace reached their ears. The market was only a couple of miles away from their house. Soon they were filing past familiar fruit carts, grain carts, vegetable booths, dairy booths, and meat stalls.

"Hmm," Zebedee muttered. "That is odd."

"What?" asked Jacobus.

"The market place is not bustling like usual," Zebedee answered.

"It's because most people are busy harvesting," explained Jacobus. "As you know, thousands of men were stationed in the south, waiting for an invasion from William, duke of Normandy, so they were unable to work on their fields much."

Fortunately, Zebedee and Jacobus remembered everything their mother had asked them to buy, and were able to find and purchase all of it, as well as some lovely grapes and dates.

After shopping, they arrived back at their parents' house to see Simon lying down on his bed with a towel on his forehead, and Hilda and Leofric scurrying about as Priscilla quietly gave orders.

"What's going on?" "What has happened," Zebedee asked everyone and no one in particular at the same time upon entering the house ahead of Jacobus.

"There you are," Priscilla said. "What took you so long? Your father is sick. Store the food in its place and come help us."

"What happened to Father?" Jacobus asked with concern after he and Zebedee put away their purchases.

"Your father just collapsed all of a sudden," Priscilla explained, trying not to panic. "When he regained consciousness, he said he felt very weak and ill."

Jacobus and Zebedee helped their mother attend to their father; Hilda and Leofric resumed their cooking and cleaning duties.

CHAPTER 2

CALL TO BATTLE

It was still dark, a couple of hours before sunrise on Thursday, September 21, 1066, when a loud trumpet call awakened all those asleep in London.

They knew this trumpet sound all too well; it was the call for battle. The trumpet was followed by a familiar voice shouting, "Prepare for battle immediately, all you warriors. Prepare to travel to Yorkshire. Be at the main gates of the city and ready to leave by sunrise." It was the voice of Ælfgar, the royal announcer.

There began to be a lot of commotion outside, and it kept increasing, with the sound of doors opening and closing, the sound of people scuttling, of metal clanging against metal, and of course the sound of people talking and shouting.

"Poor Simon. How is he supposed to rest with all this racket? There is no way he can go to battle in his condition. Forget about going all the way to York. Even if the battle was here in London he couldn't fight," Priscilla exclaimed, fearing he might be called for battle.

There was a knock on the door.

"Simon? Are you there?" a voice boomed.

Zebedee couldn't recognize it because of all the commotion outside. He opened the door to see a figure fully armed for battle, holding a lamp, standing at the door.

"Greetings, Reuben, have you grown recently?" the man at the door asked.

Zebedee finally recognized both his face and his voice. It was Ælfræd, one of King Harold Godwinson's messengers.

"No," Zebedee said, and gave a sigh. "And it's Zebedee."

"What's Zebedee?" asked Ælfræd with a confused expression on his face.

"My name," Zebedee answered, annoyed. "My name is Zebedee."

"Oh, sorry, Reuben," Ælfræd apologized, looking sincere. "Is your father home? Tostig Godwinson, King Harold's nuisance of a brother, is back, and this time with an ally, Harald Sigurdsson, king of Norway. Together, they defeated Edwin, eorl of Mercia, and his younger brother Morcar, eorl of Northumbria, at Fulford yesterday. As you probably know, the eorls Edwin and Morcar repelled one of Tostig's raids a few months ago after King Harold did the same earlier this year. But those cowardly eorls are apparently now contemplating whether they should join the other side."

It was public knowledge that King Edward would die childless because he had made an oath to remain celibate forever, and he did not recant this oath even after marrying Harold's sister Gytha and changing her name to Ealdgyth. Harold Godwinson was crowned by the witan — the king's council composed of eorls and bishops — the very next day after King Edward's death. This was unusual, especially since there was more than one contender for the throne. Harold was the witan's undisputed favorite; in addition to this, on his death bed, Edward promised him that he would be the next king of Engla Land. This greatly surprised Harold because Edward had previously promised the throne to Duke William of Normandy in the year 1051. That was the year Harold and his brothers were exiled from Engla Land along with their father Godwin; Edward did not spare his own wife, Harold's sister Ealdgyth, whom he sent to a convent as an alternative to exile.

The next year, Godwin and his sons, including Harold, strong-armed Edward to end their exile and restore them to their positions by raising a large army. At some point, Harold himself had promised to bolster William's claim to the throne of Engla Land. William was Edward's second cousin once removed The witan argued that Harold's oath to William was not valid because it was made under duress while he was William's captive. Another contender, Harald Sigurdsson, king of Norway's claim to the throne was not very legitimate, but his battle experience and the size of his army prevented him from being viewed as a joke. In addition to all these contenders, Edward had a successor based on royal lineage, his great-nephew Edgar who was still a young teenager, however, Edward and the witan wanted a military leader who could defend Engla Land from foreign contenders to the throne.

"My father is home but he is very sick, he might be dying," Zebedee answered Ælfræd, sadly. "The physicians cannot even diagnose it."

"Oh, I'm very sorry to hear that," replied King Harold's messenger. "King Harold really needs him on the battlefield. How many warriors does he have under his command? We need to assemble as soon as possible."

"Just Jacobus and Samson," Zebedee replied.

"Samson the son of Aldwulf? The war hero and former huscarl?" asked Ælfræd.

"Yes," Zebedee replied.

"Wonderful," Ælfræd exclaimed. "How many hides of land do your parents have?"

"Fifteen," Zebedee replied.

"Well, then you will need to supply another warrior; figure it out and meet King Harold outside the main city gates before noon," Ælfræd declared.

Thinking aloud, Ælfræd said, "Doesn't Tostig know when he is beaten? How many times does King Harold have to defeat him before he learns his lesson? I hope this time King Harold doesn't show any mercy to that treacherous, tyrant pretender; I hope he kills Tostig."

Tostig was the eorl of Northumbria before being exiled. He was a horrendous eorl. In fact, he was so atrocious that the Northumbrians revolted against him and were able to persuade Harold to convince King Edward to get rid of him.

After Ælfræd hurried to the next house, Zebedee ran to his mother, laughing with delight.

"I will need to go and fight in this battle," Zebedee exclaimed, trying in vain to conceal his excitement. Of course he was very worried for his father and he was very sad about his sickness, but he was thrilled about fighting in a battle.

"Don't worry, Samson started training Philip about a week ago," Priscilla replied, apparently without noticing Zebedee's excitement. "We can send Philip instead."

Zebedee was despondent on hearing that news. Philip was another ceorl who worked for Simon and Priscilla.

"Go and inform Philip and Samson," Priscilla instructed Jacobus and Zebedee.

Jacobus went to inform Samson and Zebedee went to inform Philip. Both Samson and Philip lived in London.

When Samson and Philip received the news they were shocked. Poor Philip was panic-stricken. Samson feared that such brief training was not enough to prepare the young man for battle and said as much to Jacobus.

"But, Priscilla, Philip has only been training for a little over a week, which isn't nearly long enough to prepare someone for battle," Samson said to Priscilla at her house. "Zebedee, on the other hand, has been training with Simon, Jacobus and me for a few years now just for fun. He may be a little weak and he may not have a lot of stamina, but because of his superior fighting skills, dexterity, agility, and ability to dodge attacks due to his small stature, he will probably survive longer than Philip."

"Survive longer?" Priscilla asked angrily. "What do you mean survive longer? I'm not willing to send my son to his death."

"Honestly, Priscilla, I doubt either of them will survive if they fight," Samson said, "but Zebedee would probably fare better. It wouldn't be right to send Philip."

"I won't do it," exclaimed Philip. "I'm not a thegn, I don't have to. You thegns get to enjoy more wealth even though you do less work. Well, this is how you have to make up for it. Fight to the death to defend Engla Land."

Philip was correct, ceorls were not obliged to fight. Of course ceorls who joined the army were paid for doing so by the thegns they worked for, in addition to their usual pay.

"Well, I'm not sending my boys to die," wailed Priscilla.

"You know the consequences if we don't supply another warrior," Zebedee exclaimed, exhilarated.

"You look like you want to go," Priscilla cried.

"You know I do, Mother," Zebedee replied.

"Please take care of my boys," Priscilla said at last to Samson.

"I will guard them with my life," Samson assured her.

"Thank you very much," she replied. Turning to Jacobus and Zebedee she added, "Listen to Samson; don't do anything foolish."

Zebedee, Jacobus, and Samson then briskly walked to Simon's farm outside London to get a horse for each of them to ride for the long journey that lay ahead of them. Samson mounted his horse, which King Harold had given him a couple of years prior as a reward for his bravery in battle. Having no farm of his own, Simon let Samson keep it in his stable. Jacobus and Zebedee mounted their father's horses. They then returned to London on those horses to get the equipment they needed for the battle and some food for the journey.

Priscilla cried as Zebedee put on Simon's old, small chain-mail vest. Simon's newer chain-mail vest was too big for him but the right size for Jacobus, who put it on. Simon had two small helmets which were family heirlooms. Samson, unlike most ceorls, did have a small chain-mail vest and a small helmet King Harold had given him.

"Don't fight, just hide somewhere," Priscilla cried out to Zebedee and Jacobus as they left after saying goodbye to her.

As they were on their way to the main gates of London, they saw two women walking toward them. To Zebedee's annoyance, he recognized Jacobus' fiancée Alta, followed by his fiancée, Eva, Alta's second cousin. It was Eva whom Zebedee found irritating. Jacobus and Zebedee dismounted to speak with them.

At the time, most parents in Engla Land allowed their children to choose whom they married, but that was not the case for Jacobus and Zebedee. Even though there were laws prohibiting a woman's family from forcing her to marry and prohibiting a man from marrying a woman against his wishes, the law only halted forced marriages. Arranged marriages were still common, and some forced marriages did occur among the rich and powerful, but because of the strong sense of community, the populace made it their business to stop forced marriages.

Zebedee's family was less wealthy than most thegns, however, his parents felt they would make better choices for their sons in this matter. Jacobus and Alta fell in love, therefore, they were very happy with the arrangement. Eva, on the other hand, did not seem to be very fond of Zebedee and he did not blame her. He heard that her friends made fun of her because she was engaged to a short and skinny weakling who was far from handsome. Zebedee did not let anyone outside of his family know that he was unhappy about his engagement to Eva, because he did not want to cause any trouble for his parents or make them appear in an unfavorable light.

When marriages were arranged solely by parents, it was unusual for the bride and the bridegroom to meet each other before the wedding day, but Simon and Priscilla thought Zebedee and Jacobus should become well-acquainted with their future wives before marrying them. Alta's parents and Eva's parents shared Simon and Priscilla's sentiments on the matter.

"We really missed our parents and siblings very dearly," Priscilla had explained to Zebedee. "We do not want you to go through what we went through, although we do not regret our decision. So we decided to pick your wives for you, but we let you know who you would be marrying to give you years to fall in love with each other. You see, this is the best solution."

"I strongly disagree," Zebedee had protested, but to no avail.

"Be careful Jacobus," Alta said with teary eyes. "You will come back to me, right? Remember we have to get married on the 27th of October whether you like it or not!"

They laughed and hugged. She kissed his cheek, then he kissed hers.

"Remember, this is not my first battle," Jacobus reminded her.

"Yes, I know, it is your second," she replied. "Just don't let it be your last, all right? Warriors far stronger and more experienced than you have been slain in battle before."

"All right, I'll do my best," Jacobus replied.

Eva looked at Zebedee, pouted, then looked away and said, "Hmph."

"I'm surprised you came," an amused Zebedee told her. "Are you just here to give Alta company?"

Eva was taken aback. Her expression changed from slight fear and embarrassment to anger, her face growing redder.

"My parents made me come," she answered sharply. "They told me to tell you goodbye and wish you good luck, but I'm not going to do either. I couldn't care less if you return or not. Wait, I take that back, it's not true. I hope you don't return and my parents arrange for me to marry a tall, strong, handsome man who is much richer than you are."

Zebedee laughed and remembered there had been a time when he couldn't wait to marry Eva. This was before he realized that although she was nice-looking, that was only skin deep. Zebedee thought she was the meanest person he'd ever met, and most of her meanness was now directed at him. She knew Zebedee was initially thrilled about the engagement and she still pretended to believe that he was in love with her.

At least I hope she is just pretending, Zebedee thought to himself when she first claimed not to believe him when he told her he no longer wished to marry her but was being coerced to do so by his parents.

"What's so amusing? I'm serious," she yelled, bringing Zebedee back to the present.

She seemed hurt, much to Zebedee's surprise and confusion.

"I know, that is why it's so funny," Zebedee answered and began laughing again.

She obviously hates me, so why is she upset? Zebedee pondered. *I guess she wants me to be in love with her because she wants to feel flattered. Her feelings aren't hurt, her pride is.*

"You're peculiar," she said with a sudden smile, but her smile quickly faded and she walked away in a hurry and waited for Alta at a distance.

Jacobus said goodbye to Alta and mounted his horse a few moments after Zebedee mounted his.

"I'm sorry to tell you this, but it is not going to get better after marriage," Samson informed Zebedee with an amused expression on his face. "But you two will need to keep forgiving each other. Marriage is till death do you part, as you know."

"Yes, I know," Zebedee sighed.

"You two have to decide to keep loving each other no matter what," Samson continued.

But I don't want to marry her, Zebedee screamed inside his mind.

"You know she loves you right?" he asked.

"Huh?" was Zebedee's response.

"She keeps bragging about how in love with her you are," Samson continued. "She is obviously in love with you too, even if she doesn't show it."

Zebedee's jaw dropped in shock. He did not know what to say.

How could he be so wrong? Zebedee thought but decided not to say anything.

"It is almost inevitable that you will regret getting married sometime or the other," Samson informed Zebedee. "But when you do, just remember how fortunate you are to have a wife. Most marriages are not smooth sailing like your parents' marriage is."

At least I am not engaged to a woman who I think is ugly, Zebedee reminded himself, taking Samson's advice.

Zebedee did not want to marry a mean woman who kept insulting people, especially him, but the biggest reason he did not want to marry Eva was because she did not even believe in God.

"We can't know for sure if God exists," Eva once told Zebedee in secret. Zebedee had tried to convince her that God did exist, but she responded, "What is the use of philosophical reasoning about things far beyond our knowledge and understanding?" However, she pretended to be very religious in front of everyone else apart from her family.

Alta, on the other hand, was genuinely very religious and kind. She loved the Lord. Zebedee did not think she was pretty, but he did not think she was ugly either. Jacobus thought Alta was very pretty. John and Zebedee already thought of Alta as their sister, even though she and Jacobus were not married yet. She was very kind to everyone; everyone loved her.

"When Esther and I were at the lowest point in our marriage, we asked your parents their secret," Samson informed Zebedee. "They said that God came first and each other second. They decided to love each other more than they loved their parents, siblings, friends, and even their children. And they found that as they drew closer to God they drew closer to each other."

But Eva doesn't believe in God, Zebedee thought, and cried in his heart. *How is it going to work?*

Samson, Jacobus, and Zebedee reached the city gates right before King Harold and his army left. This was the first time Zebedee saw the king fully armed and swathed in armor.

He looks quite imposing, Zebedee thought.

"Where is your father?" King Harold asked Jacobus and Zebedee.

"He is indisposed, your highness," Jacobus answered.

"He is terribly ill, sir," Zebedee continued.

"Oh, I'm so sorry to hear that," answered the king. "I hope he recovers soon. My army could use him on the battlefield, but more important, he is my friend."

King Harold's army marched on night and day. They were granted three one hour breaks for meals and a four hour break to sleep each day. When someone needed to relieve himself, he had to find a place to do so only during a break.

They were marching north to Yorkshire.

Samson, Jacobus, and I are very fortunate that we each have a horse to ride, Zebedee thought to himself, *whereas many in the army, almost all the ceorls, are traveling on foot.*

King Harold's army was mostly composed of fyrd, who were local militia or part-time battle trained soldiers. Of course it also had some huscarls. The fyrd was composed of both thegns like Simon and ceorls like Samson.

No one knew the exact numbers, as no one wasted time counting. Zebedee overheard someone say that there were about three thousand huscarls and about eight thousand fyrdmen when they left London.

Simon, Jacobus, and Samson had been part of the fyrd when King Harold's army warded off one of Tostig's raids earlier that year. According to the "five hides one warrior" law of Engla Land, every qualifying thegn needed to supply the stipulated number of warriors just once a year, however, due to the dire circumstances, King Harold commanded that they do so again.

Huscarls had long mail coats, large wooden shields, and large metal helmets as their armor. Their weapon of choice was a long handled battle-axe called a Dane axe, but they also kept a sword as their secondary weapon, as well as a javelin or two. The other thegns in the fyrd had short chain-mail vests, medium sized metal helmets, medium sized wooden shields, spears as their primary weapons, and either a seax or a sword as their secondary weapons. Usually only the wealthier ones could afford a sword or a large wooden shield.

Simon's sword, which Jacobus was carrying, previously belonged to an enemy warrior whom Simon had killed in battle. Some thegns carried a javelin or two.

There were also around one hundred archers, all of whom were thegns, and each of whom carried bows and a quiver or two of arrows; most quivers could hold twenty to twenty-five arrows. The archers did not have shields or spears, but they did carry either a seax or a sword for when they ran out of arrows and had to fight in close combat, which was rare.

The ceorls in the fyrd only had small metal helmets, small wooden shields, either an iron club or a large farming tool like a pitchfork or scythe as their primary weapons, and a sickle, small axe, or sling as their secondary weapons; those who carried a sling also carried a few pebbles in a pouch to the battlefield just in case they could not find any pebbles on the battlefield. Anyone could pick up weapons and shields that belonged to fallen comrades or slain enemies. Not all ceorls who came along were brought to fight, although the vast majority were; some were brought along to carry supplies or prepare food. The estimate of eight thousand fyrdmen did not include them because they were not part of the fyrd.

King Harold had paid some thegns to employ a few ceorls to bring along ox-drawn wagons with provisions. The oxen, the wagons, and the foodstuffs and drinks belonged to those thegns. The king had to pay them more than they would have received if they sold them in the market. There were four wagons carrying meat, butter, and cheese, two bringing vegetables, one bringing fruits, four bringing bread, and five bringing drinks.

"There isn't enough beer, cider, and mead for anyone to get drunk," announced King Harold on the way. "There may not even be a sufficient amount for everyone to drink enough till we get to Yorkshire, so when we come across a spring or river you should drink the water from it if it is fresh and looks clean. If anyone gets drunk, they shall be executed on the way and their body will be left to rot on the spot they were killed. A drunk traveler is as useless as a drunk warrior."

Anglo-Saxon adults mostly drank beer, cider, and mead. In fact, they drank more beer, specifically ale, than water. Children below the age of twelve were given diluted beer, which contained more water than beer. Even the freshwater rivers were usually too dirty to drink from because of the trash thrown into them. So Anglo-Saxons usually only drank water from springs, which were relatively clean.

"I don't understand why we don't have more archers," Samson was telling Jacobus and Zebedee during the first break. "If it was up to me, about one third to a half of the fyrd would be carrying a bow and three quivers of arrows instead of a shield and a spear. Why do our people not realize that the bow is not just for hunting? If it is effective for killing animals as large as deer and boar, why would it not be effective for striking down enemies? I know that arrows won't kill an enemy soldier if it hits his armor, but I have yet to see a man whose body is completely covered in armor, and poor warriors usually don't have chain mail vests or even helmets. Imagine how frightening it would be for an army to see a couple thousand arrows flying towards them. I also don't understand why we dismount to fight. We would be a lot more formidable on horseback."

It was customary for Anglo-Saxon soldiers to dismount and fight on foot; none fought on horseback.

Jacobus and Zebedee chuckled.

"What's so funny? I'm serious," exclaimed Samson.

"We know," Zebedee replied, "John told us the same thing once, a few years ago. And he also said that during biblical times, horses, specifically chariots and cavalry, were often considered to be a measure of an army's strength. But God told the Israelites not to trust in horses or chariots, and to trust in Him alone. Usually, if the Israelites obeyed God, He would help them defeat armies that were larger and more powerful than they were, however, if they disobeyed Him, He would hand them over to their enemies, sometimes even to those who had smaller and weaker armies. John also mentioned that bows and arrows are often mentioned in the Scripture as weapons of war."

"Do you remember John telling us how the wicked King Ahab was killed by a random arrow on the battlefield?" Jacobus asked Zebedee.

"Yes, I do," Zebedee replied.

Samson gave a chortle.

"What's so funny men?" King Harold asked while coming toward them.

"Nothing, King Harold," they all replied hastily.

They did not want to offend him by giving him tactical advice. He was the king, and they were not his advisors. They feared he might even punish them. And he was not a bad general at all, as proved by his successful military campaigns.

"Well then, stop wasting your energy with useless talk and merriment," said the king of Engla Land. "We have a long journey and then a battle ahead of us."

"Apologies, King Harold," Zebedee, Jacobus, and Samson replied almost simultaneously.

King Harold immediately bade the army to continue moving north.

"There is a good reason we dismount to fight," rang a calm voice behind Zebedee.

"Please, do tell," responded Samson with a condescending tone.

"Our horses are not war horses," the man answered. "War horses are bigger and stronger. They can gallop while carrying a warrior with lots of heavy armor, while at the same time being covered with heavy armor themselves. Without armor they will die too easily. Horses are expensive."

"What is your name, my good man?" asked Samson in a genuinely friendly manner.

"Ecgberht," he replied.

"Don't you think a man's life is worth more than a horse's, Ecgberht?" asked Samson.

"Yes, of course," responded Ecgberht, "but assuming most people will survive the battle, no one is willing to take that risk. And riding a horse into battle is no guarantee that you will survive. When someone dies in battle, what do we do with their horse?"

"The horse is taken back to their family," replied Samson, understanding the reasons.

"Exactly," replied Ecgberht. "Which will help take care of their family."

"Why not import war horses from other countries if we cannot raise them ourselves?" asked Samson.

"That was tried in the past," answered Ecgberht. "The horses were very expensive, yet they seemed to decrease the courage of their riders for some reason. The cavalry fled in battle against infantry, so our people concluded that it was just not our way to fight on horseback."

"That's understandable," Zebedee said. "Thank you for taking the time to explain, Ecgberht." Zebedee wondered if the Israelites raised their own war horses, bought war horses from other nations, or both.

On the way to Yorkshire, more local militias generously volunteered to help and joined King Harold's army. King Harold did not have to compel them to join him, they wanted to defend their king and their country.

Zebedee wondered if his friends Hreodbeorht and Clement were marching along with them. If they were, they would have joined the fyrd in London. Hreodbeorht was a strong warrior and was skillful with most melee weapons, which were weapons for hand-to-hand combat and functioned as extensions of the warrior's arms and hands. Clement was extremely intelligent, and although he seemed weaker than Zebedee, and was not very skilled with melee weapons, he was an excellent archer. Both Clement and Hreodbeorht had fought against Tostig's army earlier that year.

The few archers in King Harold's army were young lads between the ages of fifteen and nineteen. Only those who were exceptionally good with the bow would join the fyrd as archers. Naively, Anglo-Saxons saw archery as next to useless in a battle and therefore men who were twenty years old or above were ridiculed if they fought as archers. The common thought was that by the age of twenty all able bodied men should be strong enough to be useful melee warriors. Zebedee was terrible with the bow and therefore he did not join the archers. If he had, he may have been worse than useless. As much as his parents wanted him to keep distant from enemy warriors, their consciences would not permit them to send Zebedee to battle with a bow and arrows, thereby endangering the lives of the men who fought alongside him.

Only thegns could afford to hunt on a regular basis. Ceorls rarely had the time to hunt, but some found the time to do so during holidays. Anglo-Saxons hunted boar, deer, and birds utilizing the bow; they also used hunting dogs or birds of prey. The wealthier the thegns were, the more often they hunted. Simon and Jacobus hunted once each month or two, while Hreodbeorht's and Clement's parents sent them to hunt every week or every other week. Zebedee wished he could join Jacobus in his hunting expeditions, but he was stuck with the boring farm work more than Jacobus. Anglo-Saxons never hunted for sport, although they did enjoy the hunt.

The only pleasant thing about the journey to Yorkshire was the autumn scenery. The Anglo-Saxon army was moving fairly quickly, but not too quickly for them to admire God's creation on the way. It was Zebedee's first time travelling so far away from London. He was thrilled to see various kinds of trees: alder, alder buckthorn, ash, aspen, beech, silver birch, wild cherry, crab apple, dogwood, elder, hawthorn, hazel, juniper, lime, and field maple. He also saw various kinds of animals: beavers, hedgehogs, deer, squirrels, frogs, toads, newts, lizards, snakes, owls, sparrows, and robins.

The first snake he saw was approaching the army and a trio of soldiers killed it. The second snake he saw kept its distance from the army.

Zebedee recalled his parents telling his brothers and himself that owls were beautiful and magnificent creatures, and that they hoped the three of them would be able to see one someday. Both John and Jacobus had seen an owl before, but this was Zebedee's first time seeing one. Now that he had seen a couple, he knew that beauty really was in the eye of the beholder. He thought an owl's face was the ugliest thing that he had ever seen and realized he was as scared of owls as he was of snakes.

Zebedee's favorite animal was the beaver; he had no idea why.

"All right, troops," King Harold announced on the morning of Sunday, September 24, 1066, after the army had finished their breakfast. "I know we are all good Christians and we keep the Lord's day holy every Sunday, but we all need to make an exception today. I'm sure God will understand. We have to fulfill our duty and protect our country, so we will continue. We should reach Tadcaster this evening if we continue at the same pace. Once we arrive at Tadcaster we can eat a hearty meal and rest there for the night."

"Hooray!" roared the army.

"I wish we could attend church today," Zebedee heard a voice behind him say. "At least we could get some rest."

"I heard King Harold was a religious man," another voice said. "Why does he not let us attend church and join us?"

If King Harold was very religious he would not keep a mistress, Zebedee thought to himself, worried for the king's soul. *And why did he marry a woman with the same name as his mistress?*

King Harold had two wives, both named Ealdgyth, just like one of his sisters. His marriage to the first Ealdgyth did not have the blessing of the Church of Rome, so she was seen as his mistress, even though they had a few children together. Harold's formal marriage to the second Ealdgyth was for political purposes; he married her to secure an alliance with her brothers Edwin and Morcar.

The army continued their ride northward. They were given a small midday meal because supplies were low, after which all the provision wagons were empty. Usually, the midday meal was the largest of the day for Anglo-Saxons.

"Thank you, Lord, for the rivers and springs," Jacobus prayed out loud.

Because of the fresh water rivers and springs they came across, everyone had enough to drink.

When the sun was setting, and the town of Tadcaster was in view, the army cheered and rode or ran toward it, forcing King Harold to ride faster, as well.

"Halt!" one of the gatekeepers shouted. "We were just about to close the gates. Who goes there?"

"Your king does, my good man," answered King Harold.

"Your majesty!" exclaimed the gatekeepers. "Welcome to Tadcaster."

"Thank you," replied the king. "What are your names?"

"I'm Cyneweard," answered the first gatekeeper, the older of the two. "And this is my son, Deorwine."

"We have been expecting your arrival, my lord," said Deorwine, "but not so soon."

"When did you leave London, my king?" asked Cyneweard.

"Thursday morning," responded the king.

"What?" asked the astonished gatekeepers.

"How…how did you make it here so quickly…" began Cyneweard.

"We travelled night and day with little rest in between," replied King Harold.

People started coming out of their houses and cheering as King Harold rode along the main street of the town.

"All right men, buy some food and drink, consume them, and meet me back here in less than an hour," announced King Harold after they arrived at the center of the town. "And remember, anyone who gets drunk will be executed."

Jacobus bought fish, ears of corn, and carrots. Samson bought loaves of bread and some mutton. Zebedee bought buns, some beef, and some cheese. Their hunger pangs intensified at the sight of food and they wolfed down their meal. They gulped some cider after their meal. Anglo-Saxons usually drank cider in the autumn, and when they did they drank more cider than anything else; it was a good change from drinking beer every day.

"How far did we travel from London?" Zebedee asked Samson as they made their way back to the center of the town.

"About one hundred seventy-five miles," replied Samson.

"Inconceivable," Jacobus and Zebedee exclaimed together.

"What?" questioned Samson. "Did it feel like we travelled less?"

"Well, no," Zebedee answered, "but that is a long distance."

After the trio returned to the center of the city, King Harold waited for an additional quarter hour for everyone else before announcing, "I was informed about the enemy's position. They are camped at the village of Stamford Bridge, awaiting hostages from the city of York, which has surrendered to Harald, king of Norway, and my brother Tostig. We are going to camp close to York tonight. We will camp outside the city as the gates of the city will be closed and we don't want to alert the enemy. Many of our comrades in Tadcaster will join us in our fight against the king of Norway."

Everyone cheered.

They travelled nine additional miles till they came close to York and camped there for the night. Scouts were sent to Stamford Bridge to find the precise location and the size of the enemy army. The scouts returned safely, but the rest of the army was uninformed that night.

"It is not important for them to know and I want them to sleep well the night before the battle," King Harold said to his messengers.

CHAPTER 3

THE BATTLE OF STAMFORD BRIDGE

The Anglo-Saxon army marched into York as the sun was rising the next morning. They saw the gates open as they approached the city. Once inside the city, the huscarls swiftly killed the Norwegians who had come to take hostages to Stamford Bridge. King Harold then recruited a little over three thousand men from York to join the fyrd before he and his army set off to Stamford Bridge.

"Don't be afraid men," King Harold encouraged his troops on the way. "The Norwegians invaded with a force of only ten thousand men, of whom one thousand have already perished in battle against the Mercians and the Northumbrians, while we are now fifteen thousand strong."

The seniors in the army were encouraged by the familiar words of their general, who had led them to great victories before. A loud cheer erupted across the Englisc army.

"Onward!" shouted King Harold and continued leading his troops to Stamford Bridge.

They arrived at the village of Stamford Bridge about three hours before noon, descending a peat-covered moor hill. They caught Tostig Godwinson and Harald Sigurdsson's army completely by surprise. The invaders obviously had not expected King Harold's army to travel at such a rapid pace, nor to come so soon.

It was a hot and humid autumn day; the sun was blazing by the time the battle began.

I suppose it is both because of the hot weather and the unanticipated appearance of our army at this time that the majority of the enemy are not wearing any armor right now, Zebedee thought to himself. *It looks like they were relaxing and celebrating. We'll teach them a lesson about not celebrating so early.*

The Anglo-Saxons on horses dismounted and charged at the enemy. Their comrades who were on foot followed behind them. The majority of the enemy army was on the east side of the bridge, while King Harold's army was on the west side. Beneath the bridge was the River Derwent. The few Norwegian invaders scattered on the west side started to flee across the bridge with just their weapons, to join their comrades on the east side, leaving their food and beverages behind.

"Let's hope that we have enough energy left to fight," said a slightly tired Samson. "I feel sorry for those who had to travel here by foot."

"True," replied Jacobus. "There is no point in scaring your enemy only to be slaughtered by them."

Zebedee gulped. He felt anxiety welling up inside of him, making him feel weak and more tired than he already was.

There is no point in worrying, Zebedee thought to himself. *It will only make me weaker and more likely to perish.*

While running toward the fleeing enemy Zebedee spotted an enormous bird flying not very high in the sky.

"What kind of bird is that?" he asked Jacobus and Samson.

"I see it," exclaimed Jacobus. "I think that is an eagle."

"Yes," replied Samson. "Definitely an eagle. A golden eagle to be more precise. It probably came from Scotland. That is where most of them are in this part of the world."

"How can you tell?" Jacobus asked.

"The color, the size…" answered Samson.

"Oh, I see," Jacobus replied.

"Impressive," Zebedee exclaimed.

"It looks like they have fewer than nine thousand men," said a huscarl in front of Zebedee.

"Yea," added another. "I think they only have about five thousand."

King Harold's huscarls led the pursuit, followed by the other thegns in the fyrd, who were in turn followed by the ceorls. Samson was an exception; he was with the thegns.

God Almighty, heavenly Father, please help and protect Jacobus, Samson, and me, Zebedee prayed in his mind.

The bridge was only wide enough for one person to enter at a time, so there was a line of fleeing soldiers for crossing the bridge. Many Norwegians tried swimming across the river. Most of them made it across, although some fell victim to arrows from the Anglo-Saxon archers, and some drowned. Making it across was quite a feat for someone who could swim reasonably well but carried any weapons or armor, so many of them who swam across had to abandon their gear. The huscarls managed to cut down about a dozen Norwegians before they stepped onto the bridge, although a couple of the huscarls also were slain.

There was one humongous Norwegian warrior who was not fleeing like the rest. He stood a couple of feet beside the west entrance of the bridge, waiting for his comrades to flee across it. When the last of his comrades had stepped onto the bridge, he did so as well, but instead of fleeing like his fellow Norwegians, he walked backward, with his back toward his compatriots on the east side of the bridge. He came to a stop about eight feet from the west entrance of the bridge, still facing the Anglo-Saxons. Now Zebedee understood that the enemy was not retreating, they were just making a strategic withdrawal to regroup.

There he was, a lone, extremely well-built, gigantic, axe-wielding, Norwegian warrior, standing his ground and guarding the entrance to the west side of the narrow bridge with a larger than normal Dane axe in one hand and a larger than normal shield in the other.

The Englisċ army, which had previously been pursuing the fleeing enemy, paused for a few moments; they were stunned by both the bravery and size of this man. He dwarfed everyone in the Englisċ army. He was not inhumanly tall like Goliath, the Philistine champion whom God delivered into David's hands, so no one would have wondered if he had some Nephilim blood running in his veins, but he was about seven and a half feet tall.

The huscarls rushed at him with full force, one man at a time, because it was a narrow bridge, but the Norse colossus destroyed wave after wave of single huscarls. After he single-handedly slaughtered almost forty of King Harold's huscarls, it became clear that just rushing at him one at a time would not work. There was probably no man on earth who could beat this huge foe in one-on- one combat. King Harold's army clearly needed a new plan, since nearly forty elite troops had not even managed to give him a single cut. This man was holding up the Englisċ army by himself at this narrow bridge, and if the Anglo-Saxons kept charging like they had, he would be able to slaughter the entire army if he had enough endurance to keep fighting that long.

Suddenly he let out a guttural battle cry, which sounded like an animalistic roar. Every Englisċ soldier in front of Zebedee was startled, and those behind, not as much. Zebedee was more perturbed than most of his comrades around him.

"Where is Samson the son of Aldwulf?" shouted King Harold in desperation.

Samson quickly moved through the army toward the front.

"I'm here, my king," he said nervously, knowing what was coming next.

"I'm sure you've had the chance to learn his fighting pattern from what you observed," said the king. "Whatever you do, don't get hit by that colossal axe. You are our only hope, Samson."

"The Lord is our only hope, sire," replied Samson. "I cannot defeat that giant."

"What? Has the great Samson finally met his match?" sneered a clearly jealous huscarl.

"This is madness! He is not the Samson of the Bible," Zebedee exclaimed after coming forward to stand where Samson and the king were. "He may be the strongest man in all of Engla Land but he doesn't have superhuman strength."

"Are you calling your king a madman?" asked King Harold in amusement rather than anger.

"No, your highness," Zebedee replied. "My sincere apologies. That is not what I meant to imply. It did not come out right."

"My king, you saw what happened to those three dozen warriors that man slaughtered," Jacobus interjected, coming to stand closer to the king than Zebedee and Samson were.

"That enormous axe-man doesn't have superhuman strength either," King Harold replied calmly.

"I will at least need to borrow a huscarl's weapons and better armor to fight that giant axe-man," said Samson, regaining his composure.

"You can borrow his," replied King Harold, pointing at the huscarl who was mocking Samson earlier.

"What?" blurted out the huscarl. "I mean, of course."

That huscarl first lay down his shield and weapons before taking off his helmet and long chain mail vest and handing them to Samson, who put them on.

It feels good to wear huscarl gear again, Samson thought to himself as he recalled his huscarl days.

While Samson was preparing for battle, Jacobus pulled Zebedee aside and said, "Hey, Zebedee, I have a crazy idea, and it just might be crazy enough to work. Remember, brain tramples over brawn. Let's hope we can execute it in time to prevent Samson or any more of our fellow soldiers from being slain by that giant."

"Great," Zebedee exclaimed. "What do you have in mind?"

"See those small barrels over there?" Jacobus asked, pointing a little upstream on the River Derwent, which was rushing under the bridge from where the two of them were standing.

"Where?" asked Zebedee, looking in the direction Jacobus was pointing. "Oh, I see them now."

"See if you can get into one of them," Jacobus said.

Jacobus ran toward the barrels, which must have been left there by the fleeing invaders who were along the river bank. Zebedee followed him.

The barrels smelled of mead and beer. Some of them were not quite empty.

"Do you remember that hide-and-seek game we used to play when we were younger?" Zebedee asked Jacobus as he stepped into one of the empty barrels, which smelled of beer.

Jacobus laughed.

"Of course I do," he replied. "You loved hiding in barrels. It was never hard to find you before you turned nine. Good thing you are still so slim; you may be the only one here who is skinny enough to fit in this barrel."

"That is if you don't include Clement," Zebedee remarked.

"You're right," replied Jacobus, "and Clement can swim. Let's try to find him quickly and ask him if he would do it. Think about it, with a bow and arrow he can attack from a farther distance, too."

"There is no time for that Jacobus, and you know it," Zebedee responded.

"Maybe this is a bad idea," Jacobus remarked. "Samson and I can't protect you out there; you will be on your own. What if you fall into the river? You can barely swim; you'll drown for sure, and Mother and Father will kill me for making you do this. Forget it. Don't go. We'll figure out something else. Maybe we should suggest that all the archers shoot at him at once. What would he do then?"

"Well, something has to be done, and quickly," Zebedee replied. "Besides, look at the size of his shield. It should be able to protect him from a barrage of arrows that are all coming from one direction if he crouches and covers himself with it."

"But..." Jacobus began.

Instead of waiting for a response, Zebedee pushed the barrel away from the bank with his spear.

"Zebedee, no, come back," Jacobus shouted and lunged forward, reaching out his hand to grab the barrel. If Zebedee had not pushed him back with the shaft of his spear, Jacobus may have fallen into the river, however, pushing him back almost tipped over the barrel Zebedee was in.

"Ahh," shouted Zebedee, but not very loudly, as fear filled him momentarily.

"Sorry Jacobus, it has to be done," he yelled over the noise of the river.

He went in the barrel with all his gear and sailed directly downstream toward the bridge.

He saw Samson walking to the axe wielding giant before pointing at him with his borrowed Dane axe and asking with a loud voice, "What is your name, giant?"

The gigantic Norwegian warrior laughed along with many of his comrades who were in earshot.

Do they understand Englisc? Zebedee pondered.

"Julius," responded the enormous invader. "But why do you ask, knowing you will die in a few moments? Even if you are Engla Land's champion, you will fall this day."

"I am ready to meet my Maker, or at least I will be after going through the fires of purgatory for a while," replied Samson. "And for your sake I hope you are, too."

"I was created by my parents, and they were created by theirs," Julius replied in anger.

Fortunately, the river current took Zebedee exactly where he needed to go. As he sailed along he prayed in his mind, *please don't let me fall in the water, Lord Jesus, please.*

Like the gigantic Norwegian, Samson was holding a Dane axe in one hand and a large shield in the other, although when using a Dane axe huscarls usually did not use their shields. Dane axes had heavy blades and long handles, so even huscarls needed to wield them with both hands to use them effectively.

Samson was astounded when he saw Zebedee sailing on the river in a small barrel but he quickly directed his attention back to his opponent. He ran toward Julius, then stopped just out of his axe's reach. He stepped back just in case Julius swung his axe at him, which he did, and missed. Zebedee knew what Samson was doing. He was just distracting Julius so that he would not notice Zebedee.

When Zebedee was about to travel right under the large Norse axe-man, he put his shield down in the barrel, held his spear with both hands, and thrust his spear between two planks of the bridge, stabbing the humongous warrior from below with all his might to make sure to kill him.

"Ahhh!" shouted the tall troop as he let go of his axe and shield, which fell to the ground in front of him on either side. He looked down and cried like a child before falling to his knees.

Sympathy filled Samson's eyes.

The great Norwegian warrior fell to the ground on his face.

Zebedee did not have enough time to pull his spear back, as the river was flowing too quickly; he wanted to make sure to kill the Norseman while at the same time not falling into the river. Zebedee's spear was stuck in the massive man till he fell face forward and it fell into the river below.

Only then did he notice Jacobus running along the riverbank to keep up with him.

Suddenly the river current started to flow even faster, sending Zebedee toward the east side of the river.

A Norwegian ran towards the spot along the river bank where it looked like Zebedee's barrel would crash.

"O God," Zebedee desperately cried out, terrified. He was pleading with his heavenly Father, not taking His Name in vain but too scared to form words.

Before Zebedee knew it, his barrel started flowing perpendicular to the river's current and crashed onto the west bank of the river.

If my barrel were a ship, this would be called a shipwreck, Zebedee thought to himself, amused.

Jacobus helped him up from the barrel-wreck. Zebedee's shield was broken too.

"Are you all right, Zebedee?" he asked.

"Yes, I'm fine, thanks," Zebedee answered. "How about you?"

The two of them embraced each other as they laughed and cried in relief.

Thank you Lord, Zebedee prayed in his mind. *Thank you for protecting me.*

"Excellent, Zebedee, you did it, you killed him," Jacobus exclaimed.

"Who would have thought?" boasted Zebedee, convincing himself he was not boasting. "I killed the mightiest warrior on this battlefield, maybe even in the whole world!"

Jacobus patted Zebedee's back grinning, "Yes, you sure did, little brother."

He then looked behind Zebedee and laughed.

"What is it?" Zebedee asked.

"That Norwegian on the other side of the river, into whose hands you almost fell, is quite upset about being deprived of the opportunity to kill you," Jacobus responded, grinning.

"Did you see the way my barrel sailed perpendicular to the current?" Zebedee asked Jacobus.

"Yes," he replied, "and I think he did too. I heard you cry out to God, and I'm sure that man must have, as well. God is good."

Some of the militiamen came to congratulate Zebedee before going back to the battle. Jacobus followed them and Zebedee unsheathed his seax and followed him, thanking the Lord again as he went. The Englisċ army started racing across the bridge in single file. The Norse invaders were not putting up much of a resistance. The Anglo-Saxons wondered why Norwegian archers weren't shooting them.

"Here," Jacobus said after turning back to hand Zebedee his spear and his shield when they were about fifteen yards away from the western entrance to the bridge.

"No," Zebedee said. "You keep them."

"Don't bother picking up a fallen huscarl's axe," Jacobus instructed him. "It is important that you use a shield. Besides, neither of us got any practice with a Dane axe. Pick up a sword if you can't find a spear, but more importantly, pick up a shield."

Lord Jesus, please help me, Zebedee prayed desperately in his mind.

Only one weapon and one shield lay on the ground and when he grabbed them up, Zebedee found the biggest sword he had ever seen inside the biggest scabbard he had ever seen, just lying there, still attached to the colossal Norwegian's baldric, or cross-shoulder belt. He picked up the scabbard with the sword still in it but left the baldric, which was too big for him. He also picked up the huge shield. His mouth fell open with amazement at his loot.

"How grand," Jacobus exclaimed, grinning, "both the hilt and the scabbard are decorated with gold."

"Hurry up, hero," shouted a voice behind Zebedee. "We want to cross the bridge too."

The battle now continued in the meadow on the east side of the bridge after the Englisċ army crossed over to that side. King Harold's huscarls formed a shield wall about ten paces away from the enemy's shield wall; the rest of King Harold's army stood behind them. Samson was in the first row behind the huscarls, holding the large axe that had belonged to that very tall Norwegian. The shield wall was a very effective formation, sometimes called nearly impenetrable, as troops stood side-by-side with their shields almost interlocked.

"I see you had enough time to give that huscarl his weapons and armor back," Zebedee said to Samson, and laughed. "It would have been funny if you hadn't."

"I'd rather keep this axe," Samson chuckled.

Both sides tried breaching the other's shield wall without breaking formation themselves, but neither army was able to get the upper hand. Some thegns in the fyrd ran forward to throw javelins and then ran back behind the huscarls. The Norwegians did this too. The probability of injuring or killing an opponent this way was greater than the probability of being injured or killed yourself. The archers in the Englisċ army kept shooting arrows as far as they could, from behind the huscarls. Fortunately for the Anglo-Saxons, the invaders did not have any archers.

"Good fighting, Zebedee," rang a familiar voice right behind Zebedee.

"You really saved the day," said another.

Zebedee looked back to see Hreodbeorht and Clement, who had come forward to stand behind him.

"It was Jacobus' idea," Zebedee told them, "and it may not have worked if Samson had not kept that giant Norwegian distracted."

"Oh," responded Hreodbeorht and Clement simultaneously.

"Clement, why didn't you just shoot him with your arrows?" Zebedee asked.

"Well I couldn't when our compatriots were charging at him for fear of accidently hitting them instead," he answered. "Then when our side was formulating a plan, and no one was charging at him, I did shoot a few arrows at him, one after the other. I wasn't alone; several other archers joined me, but he crouched and blocked them with his gigantic shield. One of my arrows and one from another archer seemed to have cut his arms, but none penetrated him. You are a real hero, Zebedee; you, Jacobus, and Samson too."

Suddenly King Harold's Anglo-Saxon army seemed to have started retreating, slowly walking backwards. King Harald Sigurdsson of Norway saw this as a breakthrough and broke formation from his own shield wall, leading his army as they charged at King Harold's Anglo-Saxon shield wall. This proved to be a costly mistake. The Anglo-Saxons had feigned their withdrawal to trick the enemy into breaking formation. This ploy resulted in the huscarls striking down more Norwegians than they would have if the Norwegians had continued to hold their position.

"Quickly, Hreodbeorht, Jacobus, get down on all fours," Clement requested. "Please let me stand on your backs."

They complied, and he stepped onto their backs and steadied himself. He then took the second last arrow from one of his quivers, aimed it, pulled back the string with all his might, and let go. His other quiver had plenty of arrows left.

"Yes, got him," yelled Clement, jumping down.

Both armies stopped and fell silent.

"Who did you get?" Zebedee asked, impatient to know. "Tostig?"

"Harald Sigurdsson!" Clement exclaimed, gleefully. "Right in his neck. I'm glad he is so tall. He made for an easy target, ha ha!"

"How tall is he?" Hreodbeorht asked, voicing Zebedee's thoughts.

"Six and a half to seven feet tall," answered Clement.

"Harald Sigurdsson is known to have chopped off the heads of many of his enemies in battle while in a state of fury." Jacobus said. "That is why they call…called, him the mad king."

"Do you surrender now, brother?" King Harold shouted to Tostig.

"Never!" Tostig furiously shouted back.

"Attack! No mercy!" shouted King Harold.

The huscarls shifted from their shield wall formation and went on the offensive, most choosing to use their Dane axes.

Jacobus and Zebedee each fought one enemy soldier during this time.

Zebedee's opponent lunged at him with his spear. Zebedee dodged, then cut off the thumb of the one holding the spear.

"Ahhh!" his opponent cried out in pain, dropping his spear.

Zebedee took the opportunity to rush at him and pierce him through with his newly-acquired sword.

Jacobus and his opponent tried to stab each other with their spears but blocked each other's thrusts with their shields. They seemed evenly matched in strength, speed, and skill. Zebedee rushed at Jacobus' opponent from the side and pierced him through with his sword.

Samson kept slashing at the invaders, killing a few. One of Samson's casualties was Tostig Godwinson. Still, the invaders did not give up. Almost immediately after Tostig was killed, a reinforcement of about four thousand Norwegian men arrived for their nearly decimated army. These men had been guarding the ships at the coast when the battle had begun.

The huscarls quickly formed a shield wall again. The reinforcements had come running all the way as soon as they heard about the battle. As a result, many were too weary to fight. Some just collapsed from exhaustion after reaching their comrades; some of those who appeared to have fainted actually died. Therefore, the reinforcements were of little help to the invaders.

When the enemy troops began to flee, King Harold's huscarls broke out of their shield wall formation to give chase, and the fyrd followed them. While fleeing, some of the invaders turned back to fight when an Anglo-Saxon warrior had nearly caught up to them and was almost in striking distance behind them. Therefore, the fyrd engaged the enemy in combat once more.

Clement kept shooting arrows at fleeing enemies who were not too far away. Hreodbeorht and Jacobus took on an invader each, alongside each other. After running past their opponents, Zebedee swiftly swung around and stabbed Hreodbeorht's opponent from behind. This startled Jacobus' opponent, who noticed Zebedee close beside him, giving Jacobus the opening he needed to fatally pierce his opponent with his spear.

"What? You stole my kill!" yelled Hreodbeorht.

"This is a battle, not a game, child," Clement derided him.

"Whew," sighed Jacobus as he sat down on the grass. "Thanks, Zebedee. He was gaining the upper hand."

"Not a problem," Zebedee replied.

"That's it, I'm finished," exclaimed Jacobus. "They are fleeing and I am exhausted."

"This is not the first time that Norway has invaded Engla Land," exclaimed Hreodbeorht. "Let us make it their last. Let's teach them a lesson they will never forget. Besides, King Harold did say 'no mercy'. Clement, Zebedee, are you with me?"

"Yes," replied Clement.

"Actually, I am tired too," Zebedee replied, truthfully.

Zebedee, who had less stamina than Jacobus, knew that it was only through God's grace that he had not fainted with exhaustion yet.

"Besides, showing mercy is a good thing," exclaimed Jacobus.

"Come on Zebedee, this will be fun," exclaimed Hreodbeorht. "Stop copying your brother."

"I am not," Zebedee replied in annoyance.

"I will guard your back," Clement told Zebedee. "We'll let Hreodbeorht go ahead of us and I will follow behind so you should be quite safe."

"Fine," Zebedee sighed and followed them.

"Just don't get yourselves killed," shouted Jacobus as the three friends left him behind and continued pursuing the fleeing invaders.

Killing that great Norse axe-man and then three additional enemies made Zebedee feel proud, even though neither his strength nor skill were really at play. Still naïve, he had not overcome his pride.

It looks like I am a great warrior, Zebedee thought to himself.

When Hreodbeorht and Zebedee nearly caught up to two fleeing invaders, the two Norwegian warriors glanced back and noticed them. They stopped running away, turned around, and looked at their pursuers. They were about the same age, but the invaders were slightly taller.

Hreodbeorht and Zebedee engaged them in battle. Zebedee was scared because he was very tired, but his opponent seemed to be as tired as he was.

Hreodbeorht and his opponent were not as tired.

Zebedee's opponent pierced his right knee with his spear.

"Ahhh," Zebedee shouted in agony, dropping both his sword and shield, falling backward, and grasping his injured leg.

If not for Clement's arrow perforating Zebedee's opponent's neck, his spear would have impaled Zebedee, but Zebedee was too overwhelmed with pain to thank Clement for saving his life. He was crying. He then saw Hreodbeorht's opponent, who was not wearing a chain mail vest, fall to the ground with an arrow in his solar plexus.

"Hey," complained Hreodbeorht, before noticing Zebedee was injured and rushing to him.

"Are you alright, Zebedee?" Clement asked.

48

"No," Zebedee whimpered, trying to suppress his anger. "Does it look like I'm alright?"

"Sorry," replied Clement.

"I'll get Jacobus," Hreodbeorht said, and ran back to Jacobus.

"Lie down," Clement instructed Zebedee.

Clement propped Zebedee's injured leg onto one of his knees, cut off a piece of Zebedee's trousers below the injured knee, and then applied pressure to the wound with it. Zebedee cried out in pain at every movement. Clement then quickly cut off more of Zebedee's trousers and put that patch of cloth over the other one and continued to apply pressure on the wound. When the bleeding stopped, he put some of the medicinal herbs he always took with him to battle on the wound and bandaged it up.

"Thank you," Zebedee said to Clement and sighed with relief. "For saving my life and treating and patching up my wound."

"You're welcome, Zebedee," replied Clement. "I'm sorry, I should have shot your opponent earlier. I think your kneecap has been shattered; you may never walk normally again. I'm so sorry."

"Thank you Clement, you saved his life," Jacobus said, panting, when he arrived.

"I'm so glad I did," Clement replied.

"Hey, is there anything I can do to help?" panted Hreodbeorht, who came back to where Clement and Zebedee were.

"Yes," replied Clement. "Hold his leg up to help stop the bleeding."

Hreodbeorht did as instructed as Zebedee cried out in pain. Clement then immobilized Zebedee's right knee by splinting two of his arrows to the sides of his leg.

"How long can you keep that up?" Jacobus asked him. "Why not just sit down and rest his leg on your shoulder?"

"Heh, true," chuckled Hreodbeorht.

Zebedee was wondering why the Lord let this happen to him after protecting him thus far.

Why Lord? Zebedee complained to the Lord in his mind.

Then he realized how foolish it was to feel proud for killing the warriors. It was just God's protection that had kept him safe thus far. He was not a great warrior at all. But even if he were, that also would have been a provision of God, and nothing for him to boast about.

Then Zebedee recalled a conversation among Simon, Samson, and John the previous year.

"While it is not wrong to fight in defense of yourself or others, Christians should certainly not attack other countries," John had told them. "And while it is customary in every nation to pursue and strike down fleeing enemies, Christians should not, even if commanded to. We are not living in the Old Testament times anymore. We are not under the Law; we are under grace. God has called us to live by a higher standard now because He has revealed more of His mercy and grace to us than He did to the Israelites in the Old Testament. Our fight is not against people but against evil powers."

"All right," Simon had said. "That makes sense."

"It is a good thing that our wives asked us to retire from being huscarls because they were worried about us, eh Simon?" Samson had remarked. "What you said about not attacking other countries makes sense, John, but if you don't pursue fleeing invaders they will simply come back another day."

"Do you remember the priest speaking about Jesus' Sermon on the Mount after he read it to us in Latin in the Gospel? There, Jesus said those who show mercy are blessed and will, in turn, receive mercy," John had replied.

"Not striking down fleeing invaders is not merciful, it is foolishness," Samson had responded.

John then said, "Or they may remember the mercy you showed them, but even if they don't, we need to be ready to die for obeying our Lord and Savior Jesus Christ."

Zebedee realized he should have shown mercy to the fleeing invaders. They were murderers, but those who pursued them as they fled also were murderers.

But God still had mercy on me, Zebedee realized. *I just suffered a knee injury; my life was spared.* Zebedee prayed in his mind, *I'm sorry for complaining, Lord! And for pursuing the invaders, and for my pride. Please forgive me.*

Clement looked around the battlefield to see if any of the Anglo-Saxons on the ground were still alive. He found his father, Thomas, lying on the ground with a stab wound in his abdomen and a slash wound across his chest; he was bleeding to death.

"Father, no!" Clement cried as he rushed toward his father and quickly treated his wounds the best he could like he had for Zebedee.

"You should go help them, I can watch over Zebedee," Jacobus told Hreodbeorht.

"Right," Hreodbeorht said, and went to help Thomas and Clement after placing Zebedee's foot on Jacobus' shoulder.

Clement had just enough herbs and bandages left to treat and dress his father's wounds.

God please heal Thomas and me, Zebedee prayed silently.

After King Harold and his army returned, their first course of action was to take away the wounded and make sure they were treated and looked after. There were about eight thousand casualties, including about five thousand fatalities, among the Anglo-Saxons. Ecgberht was among the dead.

Samson, a battle-hardened warrior, was shaken up as he returned from pursuing the fleeing invaders, much to the surprise of his friends.

"Samson, what's wrong?" Jacobus asked.

Samson began to weep, which further astonished them.

"I'm a murderer," he exclaimed, still crying.

"What? What happened?" Zebedee asked.

"Right before I slew him, I saw terror in the face of the last invader I pursued and killed," Samson wailed. "John was right."

King Harold and his army went back to York to rest. Those who were too injured to walk were supported or carried by others.

Samson carried Zebedee's new shield, Hreodbeorht carried Zebedee's new sword, Jacobus supported Zebedee who hopped on his uninjured leg, while Clement and Hreodbeorht's father Osbeorn carried Thomas.

The residents of York graciously let a few troops sleep in each house because there weren't enough inns for them all to sleep in.

"What happened at the end of the pursuit yesterday?" Zebedee asked Osbeorn, the next morning. He knew Samson would not want to talk about it.

"Pursuit?" asked Osbeorn. "Oh, you mean us pursuing the Norwegian invaders. We chased the Norwegians all the way to their ships and killed many more before taking the survivors captive.

"King Harold made a truce with the remaining Norwegians; he sent them back on their ships after he made them promise that they would never attack Engla Land again. I was informed that about three hundred sea vessels, mostly Norwegian long ships, had originally arrived carrying the Norwegian army, but just twenty-four were required to carry the survivors back to Norway. It must have been dark by time the Norwegians started sailing back to their homeland."

CHAPTER 4

CELEBRATION AND NEWS

After a couple days of rest for the soldiers, there was a celebration in York. The citizens of York had prepared a sumptuous banquet for the king and his army.

After the feast, Gyrth Godwinson, eorl of East Anglia, and Leofwine Godwinson eorl of Kent, two more of King Harold's brothers, were discussing something with King Harold. They were in a house all by themselves with two huscarls guarding the door.

"Excuse me please," Jacobus said to Zebedee. "I'll be back soon."

Initially, Zebedee assumed Jacobus needed to relieve himself, but upon thinking about it further, he had a feeling that Jacobus was up to something – something he shouldn't be doing.

Jacobus got up, and aided by the cover of darkness, sneaked up to the house where the king and his brothers were meeting to listen to their conversation. His movements were slow but not very steady.

Despite the general lack of shrubbery in the cities of Engla Land, Jacobus found a bush very close to one of the few windows of the house where the men were conferring and decided to hide in it.

"We only have about ten thousand troops left, Harold," said Gyrth frantically. "If you let the fyrd, which is most of your army, return home now, we will only have about two thousand three hundred or two thousand four hundred huscarls to accompany you. I know that the fyrd have already fulfilled their service to you, but without them we don't stand a chance against William. We need all the help we can get, lest Engla Land falls into William's hands."

"No, that wouldn't be right," replied King Harold. "I already made this army work very hard. But don't worry Gyrth, as we go south to meet William's forces in battle, we will probably gather reinforcements again. Additionally, I will instruct the eorls Morcar and Edwin to gather their armies and meet us in London. We better hurry; who knows what William will do to the citizens of Engla Land near the coast where he will land."

"Brother," began Leofwine cautiously, "it is the Lord Jesus Christ, the King of Kings and the Lord of Lords, who puts rulers on their thrones. Now remember, I'm your brother and I love you. I'm willing to fight to the death for you unless doing so would be against the will of God. You made an oath to William; you said you would support him and his claim to the throne. Mustn't you honor your oath? If you do, won't William give you a high ranking position and great wealth? Why shed more blood and let more of our countrymen die? Why don't you send a messenger with a peace treaty ahead of you to William and then meet him yourself, welcoming him to Engla Land and handing over the throne to him? Why risk being killed in battle? But more importantly, honor God by honoring your oath."

"Brother," sighed King Harold, "I fear it is too late for that. I hear William wants my head. Besides, William is probably attacking the citizens of our country right now. He doesn't care about our people. He is not an Anglo-Saxon after all, he is a Norman. He just wants the throne, and once he gets it he will, no doubt, change our culture and oppress our people. And you know very well that I was William's prisoner when I swore that oath. It was an oath sworn under duress, and I knew that the late King Edward had already promised the throne to William. I did not know he would give it to me instead on his death bed. I must honor his wishes, and the wishes of the witan and the rest of our people. How many citizens of Engla Land want their country to be conquered and ruled by a foreigner again?"

"All right," responded Leofwine. "If William is indeed attacking civilians, I will know that you are correct and he must be stopped. Or if William says it is too late for you to surrender and that he wants your head, even though you have not even entered into battle with him yet, I will know that you are correct. But if neither of those conditions are met, my troops and I cannot go with you into battle, even at the threat of execution."

"I have already lost one brother recently," replied King Harold. "I will not lose another. Especially not one who is following his conscience. Let us go to London, my brothers, and let us see what our next move will be from there. Let us gather the remaining huscarls and the fyrdmen who are still able and willing to travel and fight, and head back to London tomorrow morning. We will return to London at a much slower pace than we came here."

At this point, Jacobus stirred apprehensively and felt his hand was getting itchy and warm. Upon moving his head back to find the source of his discomfort, he noticed that he had been hiding in a holly bush.

Suddenly, a huscarl appeared beside Jacobus and pointed his sword at him before he could abscond.

"A spy, I just caught a spy," he announced with a scowl on his face, loud enough for the royals inside the house to give heed.

"What? No!" Jacobus exclaimed. "I was just being nosy. I'm not a spy."

"Shut up and stand up, man," shouted the huscarl.

Two more huscarls arrived, pulled Jacobus up, and marched him into the house.

They pushed him to the ground in front of the three Godwinson brothers.

"What?" exclaimed the king. "He is not a spy. He is just a curious young man. Don't you recognize him?"

"Are you all right, Jacobus?" he asked as Leofwine helped Jacobus to his feet.

"Yes," Jacobus answered. "Thank you, sirs."

"My sincere apologies," exclaimed the huscarl who grabbed Jacobus, "but you shouldn't be eavesdropping like that, young man."

"I am sorry," Jacobus responded with his head down.

He was not thinking clearly because he was very frightened and ashamed.

"Why are you apologizing to me? Apologize to them," he said, briefly pointing to the Godwinson brothers.

Embarrassed, Jacobus turned to them and said, "I'm sorry, sirs."

"Why if it isn't an older brother of the young man who killed the giant!" exclaimed Leofwine.

"You are the one who told him to do it, aren't you?" Gyrth asked.

"Yes," replied Jacobus. "Although I changed my mind once he entered the barrel because he couldn't swim. But he did it anyway."

"War heroes, just like their father," announced King Harold.

"Bravo!" Leofwine said and patted Jacobus' back.

"Because of you, a lot of my troops escaped certain death at the hands of that nearly invincible warrior," the king said. "When we get back to London the two of you will be rewarded."

"Thank you, King Harold," Jacobus answered.

"Come on lad," said the huscarl. "Let's leave the nobles to their discussion."

As they were leaving, Jacobus overheard Gyrth saying, "Harold, I haven't sworn any oaths to William, and the king shouldn't risk being killed in battle. Let me lead the army while you lay an ambush in case my forces are defeated. I have a plan. While I fight against William, you ..."

"Nonsense," King Harold interrupted.

By then, Jacobus was too far away to hear anymore.

"Where did you go?" Zebedee asked Jacobus curiously.

"I was listening to a conversation," Jacobus replied honestly without being more specific.

Although his mind was racing he was very tired, so he fell asleep almost immediately.

As usual, the people in York were awakened by roosters crowing at sunrise, but then the sound of a trumpet broke the dawn.

"Prepare for battle immediately, all you warriors who are able," announced Ælfgar. "Prepare to travel to London. Be at the main gates of the city and ready to leave by noon. Everyone else, you can go back home whenever you please. King Harold thanks you for your help."

"Get up, troops," commanded King Harold. "I need all my huscarls and any other thegns who are still able and willing to travel and fight to march back to London with me today. I'm sorry for asking so much of you, but we have to protect our country from William, duke of Normandy. Everyone else, return home when you wish, and thank you for your help thus far."

King Harold spotted Zebedee limping with a crutch out of the house where he was staying. The king rode his horse toward him. Jacobus, Samson, and Zebedee were staying in the same house; Clement and Thomas in another, and Hreodbeorht and Osbeorn in another. Fortunately, the three houses were next to each other. Adam and Eve, the owners and residents of the house where Clement and Thomas were staying, also owned the house where Jacobus, Samson, and Zebedee were staying; they had leased it until their last tenant moved out.

Clement, Hreodbeorht, and Osbeorn came out at the same time from their respective lodgings. Samson and Jacobus also came out right after King Harold stopped in front of their lodging.

"Samson and the two of you seem uninjured," stated King Harold, pointing to Hreodbeorht and Osbeorn. "Would you please follow me south as I go to defend Engla Land from William of Normandy? And please bring along all the ceorls you employ to fight who are uninjured and willing to come." He continued, "Clement, you can stay to take care of Thomas, but I want you to ask the ceorls you are employing to fight for me, to follow me if they can. Jacobus, you should stay to take care of Zebedee."

Samson, Osbeorn, and Hreodbeorht wearily joined the fyrd once again after gathering their weapons and armor and saying goodbye.

That same morning, unknown to King Harold and his army, Duke William of Normandy's invasion had finally begun. William and his forces had landed at Pevensey Bay, which was farther south than London. Two messengers were sent north on horseback to inform King Harold immediately after William's ships landed.

The next morning, after their breakfast, Jacobus and Zebedee went to the house where Clement and Thomas were staying.

"Nooo!" Clement screamed as they entered. "No! You can't die!"

Clement was weeping over Thomas' body. Adam, Eve, and Jacobus rushed to him to console him, while Zebedee hobbled toward him. Suddenly, a monk wearing a black scapular over a white surplice appeared beside Clement. It was Zebedee's oldest brother, John.

Adam and Eve stepped back, stupefied, while Zebedee and Jacobus gasped, mystified.

"What?" asked Zebedee. "How…?"

"John?" asked Jacobus.

John looked around and began to ask, "Where…?"

He stopped when he noticed Clement crying over Thomas' body.

John walked to Clement, raised his eyes and hands, and prayed aloud, "Lord Jesus Christ, please bring Thomas back to life and heal Zebedee's knee."

Within a few moments, Thomas stirred, slowly rose, and sat up on his bed. Color returned to his pale face and he felt all his wounds were healed. Zebedee's knee was healed too. All of them were overcome with joy and amazement. They embraced each other, laughing and crying with gladness and praising the Lord of Heaven and Earth for His lovingkindness.

"It has been so long since we last saw you, John," Jacobus voiced Zebedee's thoughts. "And even longer since we last saw you smile. I've really missed seeing you smile. By the way, how did you just suddenly appear like that?"

"The Holy Spirit miraculously transported me here from St. Peter's Cathedral, Westminster," John replied. "Indeed I was depressed when we saw one another last because the more I've read the Bible while transcribing it[9] the last four years, the more I realized that many of the teachings of both the Church of Rome and the Church of Constantinople were made up and directly contradicted the Holy Bible. I wasn't sure what to believe.

"I spoke with the abbot about it and he told me the Scriptures are very difficult to understand, that over the centuries the clergy have been trying to understand it better. For now, I should trust what the authorities and scholars have determined.

"But then I realized that church authorities leading Christians astray was prophesied in the Bible, and our Lord Jesus criticized the Jews for following the traditions of men instead of following Scripture, which is exactly what the organizational churches are doing today. The Apostle Paul, in his Second Letter to Timothy, writes that all Scripture is inspired by God and that it is useful for teaching and for equipping us for every good work, but the clergy don't want you to read it for yourselves."

John continued, "I felt such a longing in my soul to know Scripture more profoundly, to know all the Bible holds, but there were few who could instruct me in truth and faith. When I did learn something the Scripture conveys, I verified it through comparing verses and books and by asking the Lord to help me understand correctly. I must share the knowledge I have gained."

The rest of them looked confused by John's statement. All of them were thegns who were well versed in Latin, but they never thought it was necessary to read the Bible for themselves; it was not available to them anyway.

"How did you know about my knee injury?" Zebedee asked John.

"The Lord told me to pray aloud for Clement's father, Thomas, to come back to life and for your knee to be healed," John responded. "Before I could ask what happened, He brought me here."

"How did you know it was the Holy Spirit who brought you here?" Zebedee asked John.

"Because this happened to Philip in the Acts of the Apostles," John answered.

Then, as quickly as he had appeared, he vanished.

The happy little group in the room were so dumbfounded that no one spoke for a while.

"I believe in God," Eve said, "but now I want to know more about His Word as that monk said. I hope, if you soldiers learn more, you will return to York and share your knowledge with us."

"Most assuredly," Zebedee replied, hoping he would gain the insights John had described during family visits with him.

After thanking their hosts, Jacobus, Zebedee, Thomas, and Clement packed their belongings and began riding back to London.

They tried to return the way they came but realized they were completely off track by the second day. None of them could recall the path, although they more or less knew the direction they had to travel.

They started down a road with farms on either side. Had they been in a meadow or forest or similar terrain, they could hunt animals or gather fruits. It would be wrong to steal farm animals, so they decided to temporarily halt their journey and work for a thegn on the way. The man they solicited for work let them sleep in his stable during the nights. During the days they helped his family harvest crops and cut wood. They worked hard and were paid fairly.

On Sunday the 8th of October, they all decided to accompany their employer to the church he attended since it was their belief to keep the Lord's Day holy and participate in worship. The priest briefly reminded the congregation to venerate the saints and ask them to intercede on their behalf as they have more access to God.

Jacobus was not paying much attention to the service, because he was plagued with uncertainty of them making it to London before his approaching wedding day. He was every now and then praying to the Lord Jesus Christ to help them make it back to London in time.

"When I pray to saints my prayer requests are never granted," Zebedee told his companions. "I think praying to saints or even asking them to intercede on our behalf is one of the false teachings of the Eastern and Western churches. God feels uncomfortably distant when I do such things. Only God can truly understand my heart, so why shouldn't I pray to Him directly every time?"

All three of them agreed with Zebedee, saying that it was the same in their experience.

That same day, they decided to continue on their way to London, as they had earned enough food for the rest of their journey. The thegn gave them directions to London before they left.

That Thursday, as they were nearing a fork in the road, they saw a group of crudely armed ruffians, one of whom was on a horse blocking both paths. When they got off the road to avoid them, those men followed suit, and the one on horseback approached them, stopping twelve to thirteen paces away from them.

"Hand over everything you have except the clothes you are wearing and no one has to get hurt," demanded the leader of the gang.

"We can give you our weapons and armor, but nothing else," explained Thomas. "We need the rest to go back home."

"How can we defend ourselves without our weapons and armor?" Jacobus impatiently whispered to his companions.

"I'm not going to ask again," roared the gang leader, as his companions tried to form what could only be described as a poor excuse for a shield wall and pointed their pitchforks and scythes at Zebedee and his companions. "My friends and I need food and money to survive. Hand it all over or die. Look around. You are outnumbered, fools"

"I'm going to get married to Alta on the twenty-seventh," yelled Jacobus. "Neither you nor anyone else is going to stop me."

Even Zebedee couldn't remember the last time he had seen Jacobus so angry.

"Wait," shouted Thomas with a fearful voice. "Jacobus, he is correct, we are only four people. We can't take on seven men. Even if we do win somehow, how many of us will be left alive? Are you willing to risk even one of us dying? So what if your wedding is delayed a few days? Have faith! God may even help us make it on time."

"Wise man," snarled the leader of the bandits. Then to Jacobus he said, "Listen to him, boy, or you won't make it to your wedding at all."

"I have faith that God will help us win without any of us dying here today," Jacobus stated emphatically to both his companions and the bandits. Then, addressing the bandits alone, he said, "Back off if you know what's good for you."

They laughed at Jacobus in mockery. After a few moments the leader stopped laughing and raised his left hand; they all followed suit. He then pointed his pitchfork towards Jacobus and his companions and shouted, "Attack!"

"Wait!" yelled Clement, who had an arrow aimed at the leader of the bandits. "Don't be daft, I am an excellent shot."

"Wait!" yelled the leader of the band of thieves. "Let them pass."

"You're right," exclaimed one of the other bandits, as it dawned on them that the thegns were better armed and seasoned warriors. "It isn't worth it."

"What drove you to become thieves?" Zebedee asked them.

"We were tired of working so hard six days a week just to survive," answered the leader of the band of robbers. "We wanted an easier life for ourselves and our families."

Zebedee was wondering whether he should give them his large sword and large shield so they could sell them and buy food for themselves; he was hoping it would convince them to start making an honest living, but upon hearing this, he decided otherwise.

"Do you really think it is worth the risk of injury or even losing your lives?" Zebedee queried. "And don't you have any fear of God? What do you think will happen to your souls once you die?"

"None of us believes in God any longer," shouted the leader of the bandits as they scurried away on the road Zebedee and his companions had come from.

On the afternoon of Monday, October 16, Zebedee and his companions arrived in London, having returned the horses to their stables before entering the city. They were not surprised it was raining. Dark clouds had covered the sky the night before, veiling the stars from sight.

The streets were empty. Some people looked at them from their houses as they passed by. The stores were empty, too. Finally, someone shouted from their house, "Hurry to your homes, the Normans are coming!"

"What?" Zebedee asked but received no response.

He and his companions looked at each other with confused and worried expressions.

Jacobus and Zebedee bid farewell to Thomas and Clement as they parted to go to their own dwellings. They all rushed to their families.

As Jacobus and Zebedee approached their parents' house, Simon and Priscilla saw them from inside, rushed outside, and whispered loudly, "Hurry inside," while motioning with their hands.

Jacobus and Zebedee did as they were instructed. When they were all safe inside, Simon and Priscilla hugged Jacobus and Zebedee, and kissed their cheeks.

"Thank God you are back home safe," exclaimed Priscilla joyfully, through tears.

"What is happening?" Zebedee asked. "Why are you two crying?"

"Yes," said Jacobus. "And where are King Harold and his army?"

"We just received news last night that King Harold and his army were defeated by William of Normandy and his army," Simon responded, sniffling. "The fyrd fled after King Harold was killed by an arrow. The huscarls kept fighting out of loyalty to Harold. We lost about four thousand troops."

Zebedee and Jacobus sobbed silently for Engla Land and for the late King Harold.

"Oh, Father," Jacobus suddenly exclaimed with happiness in his voice, "it's nice to see you have recovered. I prayed for you two every day."

"Yes, it is nice to see you on your feet again, Father," Zebedee said.

"Thanks boys," Simon replied. "I am all better, by the grace of God. I was sick until the day before yesterday. I never thought I would say this but thank God I was sick."

"When we heard Zebedee was too injured to travel back home we were very worried," Priscilla said. "We kept praying for you, and God brought you back to us safely."

"King Harold arrived here on the sixth with his surviving huscarls and some fyrdmen from the battle in Yorkshire, and some more fyrd that he gathered on the way back from York," Simon informed Jacobus and Zebedee. "Your mother and I were worried when they told us you didn't return with Harold because you sustained a knee injury. By the way, how is Clement's father, Thomas? We heard he almost died."

Jacobus and Zebedee exchanged glances and laughed. This made their parent's look at each other in confusion.

"What's so funny?" Simon bellowed.

"He died the day after King Harold left York," Zebedee replied, at which Simon and Priscilla gasped.

Priscilla covered her mouth and then exclaimed, "Poor Clement and Abigail!"

Abigail was Clement's mother.

"But…" Zebedee tried to continue.

"That is not funny," thundered Simon. "What's wrong with you, sons?"

"But God made John suddenly appear there and he prayed for us and God healed Thomas and brought him back to life and healed me of my injury. After talking with us for a while, John vanished," Zebedee rapidly finished before anyone else interrupted him.

"Huh?" Simon and Priscilla asked in unison. "What?"

"Slow down, Zebedee," Priscilla said. "You were talking too fast. I didn't understand anything you said, apart from the words 'God' and 'John' and 'Thomas.'"

Jacobus repeated what Zebedee said slowly and clearly.

"Seriously," Simon said as he and Priscilla looked at each other in disbelief. "What really happened?"

Jacobus and Zebedee laughed again. "It is all true," they answered together joyfully.

"Look at my knee," Zebedee said, pointing to his healed knee exposed by his ripped trousers.

"I can't believe it; it's incredible," exclaimed Priscilla.

"Let's go see how Thomas is doing and ask him for ourselves," declared Simon.

Simon and Priscilla were awestruck; it was so amazing they still had difficulty believing it. They left for Thomas' residence right away, ignoring all precautions about safety in their excitement. Jacobus and Zebedee followed.

"Father," Zebedee said. "You didn't tell us how King Harold prepared for battle."

"Later, son," he said impatiently. "This is more important. God brought a dead man back to life in our day."

"I always knew John would be a great man of God," Priscilla exclaimed.

"Greetings! Welcome," Thomas greeted Simon, Priscilla, Jacobus, and Zebedee with a smile after opening the door and stepping aside to let them in.

Thomas hugged Simon, Jacobus, and Zebedee while Abigail embraced Priscilla joyfully. Clement came and greeted the guests after preparing a place for them to sit.

Thomas' and Abigail's male thralls were cooking while their female thralls were preparing the table and dishes to serve the food.

"So," began Thomas, "did Jacobus and Zebedee tell you what happened in Yorkshire during and after the battle at Stamford Bridge?"

"That is what we came to verify," Simon responded. "They told us an extraordinary story about John suddenly appearing in front of them and then praying, and you being healed and brought back to life and Zebedee being healed. Then they apparently had a short conversation with John but didn't go into detail, and then John disappeared."

"It is all true, my friend," Thomas confirmed. "Every word of it, but the conversation is very important too."

"We were going to mention that eventually," Zebedee told Thomas. "They were already overwhelmed by the miracles. We wanted…we needed…them to believe us about that first. If it wasn't for the miracles, I would have concluded that all the seclusion of his way of life had driven John insane."

"Hmm, very true," Thomas replied thoughtfully.

"They didn't tell us what happened at the battle though," Priscilla stated. "King Harold told us they used their wits to kill an unbeatable giant of a man."

"That is true, too," Thomas exclaimed, "but first we need to talk about what John said."

"Before we get into that serious topic," began Clement, while giving the guests some soup and bread, "I think we should finish this less serious topic."

The rest chortled because they agreed with Clement.

The aroma from the soup wafted into the air. The soup had peas, onion, carrot, and chicken, a typical Anglo-Saxon preparation. The war heroes, who hadn't eaten fresh warm home delicacies for days, ravenously attacked the food.

"All right, son," responded Thomas. Then, facing Simon and Priscilla, he said, "There was this extremely tall Norwegian man guarding the bridge. He was about seven and a half feet tall. He kept massacring our huscarls. He killed roughly forty of them by himself. The bridge wasn't wide enough to overwhelm him with sheer numbers. Only one man could fight against him at a time. His shield was large enough to protect him from serious injuries from arrows. It looked hopeless. Jacobus was too big to fit in the barrel. Zebedee followed Jacobus' plan against Jacobus' wishes and sailed in a tiny barrel in the river toward the point on the bridge where the giant Norse axe man was stationed. Samson distracted him so Zebedee could approach him unnoticed and impale him with his spear from under the bridge. Only after Zebedee killed the giant did anyone, apart from Jacobus and Samson, notice him in the barrel sailing on the River Derwent."

"Zebedee," Priscilla scolded her youngest son. "Why would you take that risk? What if you'd fallen into the river? Did you forget you can't swim?"

"That is why I changed my mind," Jacobus stated. "I remembered he couldn't swim."

"Well, someone had to do it. Now that it is out of the way, let's move on to the more serious topic," Zebedee said, not wanting to be scolded anymore.

"Oh," Jacobus exclaimed, "I was planning on dropping Zebedee home and then going to see Alta. I was distracted because of all the excitement about the impending Norman invasion. You three tell them what happened. I must go. I'm sorry."

"Thank you very much for your hospitality," Jacobus said to Thomas and his family before going out into the rain.

"Zebedee, aren't you going to see Eva?" Clement asked.

"No," Zebedee replied, unhappily.

"What's wrong?" asked Clement. "You two don't seem very fond of each other. If I didn't know any better, I would think that your parents are forcing you to marry her."

Simon, Priscilla, and Zebedee looked at each other nervously.

"Don't be…" Zebedee was about to say "ridiculous," but Abigail interrupted him.

"Zebedee, did you know that you have been granted your own house and land?" she asked. "You can be fully independent now."

"What are you talking about?" asked Zebedee.

"You haven't told him yet?" Abigail asked Simon and Priscilla.

"No," Simon responded. "With so much going on we forgot about it." Turning to Zebedee he said, "King Harold rewarded you, Jacobus, and Samson with animals, a thrall or two, and ten hides of land each. And you and Jacobus have also been given a house each. The ceorls who used to work on those lands for the previous owner have agreed to work for you. The previous owner of the land died in the battle at Stamford Bridge without a living heir, as did the ceorls who owned the other houses. Zebedee, you have been given the thegn's house."

Hearing this, Zebedee thanked Thomas, Abigail, and Clement for their hospitality and left their house in a hurry.

"Zebedee, wait a minute," Priscilla protested, after opening the door right after Zebedee left. "Think about what you are doing."

But Zebedee already knew exactly what he needed to do.

He briskly walked to his fiancée's parents' house.

He knew Clement and Thomas did not need his help to describe what happened at Yorkshire and what John had said. Right now, his main concern was breaking his engagement to Eva.

Zebedee knocked on the door of Eva's parents' house. Eva opened the door, and to Zebedee's surprise, hugged him while squealing with delight, "My brave giant slayer."

"What? Who are you?" he asked her.

She giggled.

"Listen, I know I haven't been very nice to you," she began, "but that is because I thought you were inferior to the others. I'm sorry for all the rude things I said about you."

"I forgive you," Zebedee responded, bewildered. "So you like me now, just because I killed a really big and strong man?"

"Yes," she grinned.

Zebedee laughed.

"What is so funny? Stop laughing at me," she protested, putting her hands on her hips and frowning.

Zebedee ignored her question because he did not know how to answer it. Instead, he asked a question of his own, "Wait, how did you know I killed a very tall warrior?"

"Everyone knows about it," she exclaimed. "King Harold praised you, Jacobus, and Samson for what you did in the battle at Stamford Bridge. He announced it to the whole city upon his return, before giving the three of you your own property."

"Oh," Zebedee replied. "Eva, I still don't want to marry you, and now that I don't need to be afraid of being kicked out of my parents' house, I'm breaking our engagement. I'm sorry. Really, I'm very sorry."

"Why?" she shrieked. "What is wrong with me?"

"I won't marry a non-Christian," Zebedee replied, frowning.

"But I am a Christian," she exclaimed. "I was baptized when I was a baby just like you were, and I usually go to church on Sundays."

"So what?" exclaimed Zebedee. "You didn't have a say in your baptism and your parents make you go to church because they are religious. You don't even believe in God. How can you say you're a Christian when you don't believe in Christ, who died on the cross for your salvation?"

"Prove to me right now that there is a God and that Jesus is God," she demanded. "Give me reasons I should believe what the Church teaches!"

"The day after the late King Harold left York, Jacobus, Clement, his father, and myself witnessed miracles," Zebedee answered.

"What miracles?" she asked, astounded, but skeptical.

"Thomas, Clement's father, succumbed to the injuries he sustained in the battle at Stamford Bridge and died, and I sustained a knee injury," Zebedee answered. "John suddenly appeared and prayed, asking God to bring Thomas back to life and for my knee to be healed. Thomas came back to life and both of us were completely healed almost instantly."

"Prove he died," she said, before going back inside, shutting the door, and starting to wail loudly.

Poor Eva, Zebedee thought to himself. *I feel very sorry for her, but I can't marry her. I won't do it.*

As Zebedee turned to go back to Clement's house, he saw Jacobus and Alta walking together, holding hands, and smiling.

"Who is crying?" Jacobus asked as they came closer to where he stood outside Eva's door.

"Eva," Zebedee replied.

"Why?" asked Alta, with concern. "What happened?"

Zebedee felt awkward, so he just responded, "I'd prefer it if you asked her yourself."

"Don't be long, Alta," Jacobus said to his fiancé.

"Only as long as it takes," she replied.

As Alta knocked on the door, a big commotion started some distance behind Jacobus and Zebedee, coming from the main gate of the city.

Jacobus yelled to Alta, "Stay in Eva's house till I come fetch you."

Jacobus and Zebedee went towards the sound of the uproar. To their relief, it was not the Normans but the returning Anglo-Saxon army, or what was left of it anyway.

"The Normans aren't coming to London yet," one trooper announced. "They went in a different direction. William probably wants to suppress all possible opposition before coming to London."

Jacobus and Zebedee searched the returning soldiers for their friends. Near the back of the remnant of the once-mighty Anglo-Saxon forces, they found Osbeorn, walking slowly with his head down and tears streaming down his face.

"Osbeorn, what happened?" Jacobus and Zebedee asked.

"Are you all right?" Jacobus asked.

"Where are Hreodbeorht and Samson?" Zebedee asked.

"Dead," he responded, hearing his son's name along with Samson's. He fell on his knees sobbing, with his face in his hands. "Both of them perished in the battle against William's forces."

"I'm so sorry to hear that," Jacobus and Zebedee said together.

Jacobus and Zebedee started weeping, tears slowly running down their cheeks. They tried to hold them in but they could not. Zebedee, who was closer to Hreodbeorht, cried more than Jacobus did. They wiped their tears away with their hands. Both offered silent prayers for the repose of the souls of their comrades.

When Osbeorn composed himself a little, Jacobus and Zebedee helped him to his feet and walked him to his house. They decided to stay with him, his wife Sarah, and their children for a while, to try to comfort them, even if just a little.

"The Norman army and their allies were between Caldbec Hill and Telham Hill, which are about a mile to the north of the town of Hastings," Osbeorn began. He continued, "King Harold tried to surprise them early in the morning, but apparently, we were spotted before we got there. Maybe by William's scouts. Our army entered into a defensive shield wall formation on Caldbec Hill. The huscarls were in the front, forming the shield wall. We had about ten thousand troops and they had about eleven thousand. Before leaving Yorkshire, Harold had asked the eorls Edwin and Morcar to come along with their troops to assist him, and they said they would, but they did not. Oh why didn't they come?" He began weeping again.

When his weeping eased, he continued, "Almost all of our troops were regular infantry; we only had a few archers, as you know. They had about five thousand regular infantry soldiers, three thousand archers, and three thousand lancers."

"What were their lancers like?" Zebedee asked.

"Think of a huscarl with a long spear instead of an axe, riding a very large and powerful horse," Osbeorn replied.

"Oh, what a sight," Jacobus exclaimed. *Based on Ecgberht's description I thought William's cavalry would have more armor than huscarls,* Zebedee thought to himself.

"How much armor did their horses have?" Zebedee inquired.

"Their horses? None." Osbeorn answered.

I know armor is not cheap, but neither are those horses, Zebedee thought to himself, unimpressed by what he heard about the Norman cavalry so far. *I guess Ecgberht was referring to cavalry in more wealthy countries.*

Osbeorn continued, "The Norman infantry was just as heavily armored as the cavalry and they, too, had long spears. Among their archers, many used mechanical bows called crossbows; they shot arrows by simply pulling a trigger. At the beginning of the battle, their archer's shot at us to little avail; most of their arrows either missed us completely or hit our shields. Our shield wall was as effective as usual. The next wave of attack that Duke William deployed was his infantry of spearmen, but they too couldn't do much. Our army kept throwing javelins, small axes, and even stones at them as they ascended the hill to meet us in battle. Next, William himself lead his cavalry, but they too failed to break our shield wall because they had to ascend up the hill while the Anglo-Saxon army had the advantage of having the high ground. Gyrth hurled his javelin and fatally wounded William's horse and it fell on its side. Some of William's horsemen then surrounded him as others helped him up. He was swiftly taken behind the frontlines. Someone somewhere shouted, 'Duke William is dead,' and the invaders began to retreat, but several moments later William, who had mounted another horse, rode up to near the frontlines shouting, 'I live! I live! Stand your ground! I shall conquer this land,' or at least that is what I heard from someone. Before the battle, Harold ordered us to stay in position unless he said otherwise, but Gyrth and Leofwine began to pursue the enemy army. Some of our troops followed them. William's forces turned around, hemmed in their pursuers, and inundated them. Gyrth and Leofwine were killed almost instantly. Some who were closer to the front said that William killed Gyrth. Some thegns from the fyrd had to join the shield wall because we lost a lot of huscarls."

"Both sides agreed to take a break at noon," Osbeorn said. "We rested and ate our midday meals. The heads of the armies probably planned their next moves, and after the short break the Normans and their allies used more or less the same assault tactics. Again they failed to break through our shield wall; again they feigned a retreat, and again some of our troops fell for it and began to pursue them, only to be killed. At least another of Duke William's horses was killed right under him during the battle."

Everyone was pleased to hear that bit of news, but their tears continued flowing. Osbeorn continued, "Then William ordered his archers to shoot our troops in the rear lines, the poor fyrdmen. This was very successful of course, as many of them had very little, if any, armor. Most of them didn't even have shields. At the same time, William's cavalry and regular infantry assaulted us from the sides and the front. Our army was now small enough for William's forces to surround and obliterate our forces. They nearly surrounded us, leaving a gap at our rear, and began to overwhelm us. King Harold was fatally injured by an arrow to the eye and a Norman on horseback then stabbed him with his spear to kill him quickly. Once news of the king's death spread, some of our countrymen began to either flee or surrender. Samson, Hreodbeorht, and I fled along with the rest of the fyrd. King Harold's huscarls kept fighting the Norman army. Some Normans began pursuing the fleeing fyrd. Samson was killed by an arrow to the back of his neck as soon as he began to flee. Hreodbeorht and I were right next to him when he fell. Hreodbeorht pushed me out of the way of a charging mounted soldier as we were fleeing to our horses and was therefore impaled by his spear instead of me."

He paused, crying, "Oh my son," and tried vainly to fight back more tears before continuing. "That mounted warrior's horse then trampled him. I mounted my horse and fled along with the rest of the remaining fyrd. Most of us hid in some woods during the night because we were exhausted."

After saying farewell to the late Hreodbeorht's family, Jacobus ran to fetch Alta from Eva's house and accompanied her to her parents' house, while Zebedee went to Clement's parents' house, where Jacobus joined him later. Simon and Priscilla were still inside.

Soon after Jacobus arrived at Clement's residence, everyone inside the house heard a procession outside repeatedly shouting, "William is not our king, Edgar the Ætheling is our king. Long live the king."

All those inside the house went out briefly to see the parade and then went back inside the house. Zebedee was surprised at how little all of them, including himself, cared about who the next king of Engla Land would be.

After bidding farewell to Clement and his family, Simon, Priscilla, Jacobus, and Zebedee went to console Samson's family and stayed with them for a couple of hours before heading back home.

"Zebedee, what were you thinking?" Priscilla asked. "Go and beg Eva to take you back."

"No!" Zebedee replied adamantly. "I will not marry an unbeliever."

"Maybe your faith will persuade her to believe in the Lord too," Simon said. "Maybe you can show her the truth. Did you tell her about the miracles?"

"Yes, I did tell her," Zebedee answered, "but she still does not want to believe."

"Give her time," Priscilla pleaded. "Do you really think that you could easily win the heart of any woman who has her eyesight? You are neither strong nor smart, neither handsome nor rich. I'm sorry to say this son, I love you too much to let you live alone."

"Your mother is right, Zebedee," said Simon, "although I wouldn't know how to judge how good you look."

Zebedee knew his parents were only being honest and trying to help him. They wanted what was best for him. He didn't doubt their love for him, but he did doubt their wisdom and was upset with them.

"I know you well, Zebedee," Priscilla continued. "The main reason you don't want to marry her is because she is not beautiful. Your standards are too high. Your self-esteem is too high. What do you think of yourself? We didn't arrange for you to marry someone ugly."

"That is not true at all," Zebedee protested to her accusation of him being very shallow and proud. "I don't care about appearance as much as you think I do, and my self-esteem isn't high. Anyway, Mother, do you remember saying that one of the reasons you fell in love with Father was because he was the most handsome man you had ever seen?"

"What, really?" Simon asked Priscilla excitedly. "You never told me that you think I'm the most handsome man you have ever seen."

Priscilla sighed and said, "Zebedee, I don't think you will get married if we don't arrange a marriage for you, and lots of parents declined to let one of their daughters marry you after thinking about it. Obviously their daughters were unwilling to marry you."

"I would rather become a monk than marry Eva," Zebedee replied. "And my standards are not nearly as high as yours."

"Then who will take care of you when you are sick and when you grow old?" Priscilla asked.

"You need to think of the future, son," Simon added.

"I will take care of myself," Zebedee replied, "or die trying."

"Zebedee, arranged marriages usually turn out better since parents are wiser and more knowledgeable than their children," Priscilla said.

"Do you two regret marrying each other instead of marrying who your parents wanted you to marry?" Zebedee asked his parents, knowing what their answer would be.

"No," Simon and Priscilla replied simultaneously.

"But we are an exception," continued Priscilla. "You should have been thankful Eva was either willing to marry you or forced into the engagement by her parents. They are religious and they know that you are too. They said they hope you can convince their daughter to come back to God."

"I can't," Zebedee answered. "I tried and I failed."

CHAPTER 5

ZEBEDEE'S PROPERTY

The next day, before sunrise, Simon and Priscilla woke up Jacobus and Zebedee to take them to their new houses and farms. Jacobus' house was in London, while Zebedee's house was on his land outside the city. Jacobus' and Zebedee's farms, which were right outside the city, were next to each other. They arrived at Jacobus' farm first.

"Good morning, Arthur," Simon said to one of the ceorls on Jacobus' farm. "This is my second son, Jacobus."

"Good morning, Simon," Arthur replied, taking a break from harvesting beans.

Then, turning to Jacobus, he said, "Nice to meet you, Jacobus."

Arthur was clearly struggling to keep his eyes open and his head up just like the other ceorls working away on the farm.

"Good morning, Arthur, and good work so far," Jacobus replied.

"Arthur is the head of the workers on this farm," Simon informed Jacobus.

"Oh, I see," Jacobus said, turning to face Arthur again. "Starting tonight I want you all to get an additional hour of sleep. You can all disperse an hour earlier in the evening. I won't reduce your pay."

"Thank you, sir," Arthur exclaimed.

"Ælfsige," Arthur called to a young man around Zebedee's age but a little taller. "This is Jacobus, the new owner of this property. He said we can leave work one hour earlier than usual and still get the same pay. Go tell the others."

Ælfsige ran to the other workers and continued to relay the news. Cheers rose throughout the farm.

"The late King Harold put Arthur in charge of the rest of your ceorls and also your thrall," Simon explained to Jacobus.

After leaving Jacobus at his farm, Simon and Priscilla took Zebedee to his farm.

When they arrived at the border of Zebedee's farm, a man came to meet them. Zebedee assumed that he was the ceorl in charge of the rest of the ceorls who worked for him, and he was right.

"Zebedee, this is Angus," Simon told Zebedee. "He is in charge of the rest of the ceorls who work for you."

"It is nice to finally meet you," Angus exclaimed. "The man who killed the Norse giant."

"Thank you," Zebedee responded, vainly trying to hold back a grin. "It is nice to meet you too, Angus. It was my brother Jacobus' idea; I just happened to be small enough to fit in a small barrel."

"Your whole body fit in the barrel?" he asked.

"No, I was standing," Zebedee replied.

The four of them laughed.

"All right, Zebedee," Priscilla said, "Angus will show you your property. Good bye, son. God be with you."

After Simon and Priscilla left, Angus gave Zebedee a tour of his rye farm.

After Zebedee inspected the farm and met all the ceorls working on it, Angus showed him his animals. Zebedee owned horses, pigs, goats, and chickens. A middle-aged man and a young woman who looked like she was Zebedee's age were taking care of his animals.

That young woman is the most beautiful woman I have ever seen, Zebedee thought.

When the man and woman saw Zebedee and Angus, they came to them immediately.

"Dermont, Cleena," Angus said to them, "this is your new owner, Zebedee."

"Zebedee," said Angus, "these are your thralls. This is Dermont and this is his daughter, Cleena. They live in the hut that is behind your house."

"It's nice to …" Dermont began.

"Nice to meet you," Cleena interrupted as she stepped in front of Dermont to shake Zebedee's hand first. She looked at him the same way that young unmarried women looked at Jacobus before he was engaged, and at John before he started his vocation and shaved the top of his head to symbolize his rejection of earthly vanity.

Could it mean she fancies me? Zebedee wondered. *Does that mean she thinks I'm handsome? No, that's highly unlikely.*

"It is nice to meet you, too," Zebedee replied, too deep in thought to smile back.

"I heard you injured your knee," Dermont said. "You seem fine now. That was a rather speedy recovery."

"Yes, it was completely healed," Zebedee responded with a smile. "Thanks for asking. Did King Harold tell all of London everything about me?"

The three of them laughed.

"Indeed," Angus replied.

"Wait," Dermont said. "How could your injuries have healed so quickly?"

"A miracle," Zebedee informed him. "God brought my oldest brother John, who is a monk, to our location. John prayed and asked God to heal us and bring my friend's father back to life, and God did."

"Really?" Cleena asked with widening eyes. "A miracle, indeed."

"That's amazing," Angus declared. "John must be a great man of God."

"Wait a minute," demanded Dermont. "I don't believe in your God. Why should I believe you?"

"Which god do you believe in, then?" Zebedee asked, perplexed.

"The gods of my ancestors," Dermont answered.

"They are Britons," Angus explained to Zebedee. "They are not Anglo-Saxons like us. Some still haven't converted to Christianity."

Britons were the inhabitants of Engla Land before Angles, Saxons, and Jutes arrived, and gradually started taking over. Many Britons were subjugated.

Zebedee's heart sank because he knew that he could not marry a pagan, nor did he wish to.

"Well, the truth is the truth regardless of what you believe," Zebedee replied frankly.

"I believe you," Cleena told him.

"No, you don't," scowled Dermont.

"Who created the universe?" Zebedee asked Dermont.

"The gods, I suppose," replied Dermont.

"Do you believe your gods always existed?" Zebedee asked.

"No," Dermont responded.

"Who created them then?" Zebedee asked.

"I don't know," Dermont shrugged. "Perhaps the universe?"

The expression of realization on Dermont's face made it clear that he immediately realized the folly in his answer; Angus and Zebedee tried to suppress their laughter.

"No," Dermont said. "I don't know."

"It is impossible for anything humanly conceivable to have always existed," Zebedee began. "Even common sense tells us this."

"Yes," Dermont replied. "I never thought about it in that way before, but you are absolutely right."

"If there was a time when nothing existed, then everything must have been created, because things can't just come into existence by themselves," Zebedee continued.

"Exactly. Where did the creator god come from if nothing could have always existed and things can't suddenly come into existence?" Dermont responded confidently.

"Exactly," said Zebedee. "The only logical conclusion is that the Creator always existed. Which is only possible if the Creator is absolutely, infinitely perfect in every way. Which means He is eternal, omniscient, omnipotent, omnipresent, and more, and there can't be more than one all-powerful Being because that would imply that neither can stop the other; that would imply that neither is all-powerful. So the only logical conclusion is that there is one and only one God, who is the Creator and Ruler of everything."

"That's astonishing," all three of them said.

"What a wise young man," Dermont exclaimed. "How old are you?"

"Seventeen," answered Zebedee.

"Me too," Cleena exclaimed.

"Where did you learn this?" Angus asked Zebedee, patting his back. "I have never heard any magistrate giving such a logically sound proof of God's existence."

"I…umm…actually thought of this myself," he explained shyly, while looking at the ground.

"Well," said Dermont, "Jews and Saracens also teach there is only one God. How do you know which god is the true God? Maybe all three of you are wrong."

"Christians and Jews have the same God, although non-Christian Jews won't accept this statement," Zebedee responded. "The God of the New Testament is the God of the Old Testament. Jesus Christ is the God of the Bible, and since the non-Christian Jews don't believe in Him, they don't believe in their own God. The deity of that Saracen religion is not the God of the Bible."

"But how do you know the Saracens are wrong and you are right?" Dermont asked.

"Ever since I understood that I'm a sinner who deserves death and hell, and that Jesus Christ suffered and died on the cross for my sins, I accepted

Him as my Lord and Savior. That means I have a personal relationship with Him," Zebedee answered. "And I already told you about some miracles my God performed before my very eyes. He has done many more things in my life I haven't told you about."

"Right," Dermont responded. "This will certainly give me something to think about."

"All right," said Angus. "It is time for you two to get back to work."

"Will I see you here tomorrow?" Cleena asked Zebedee, smiling.

"Umm…Yes, I think so," Zebedee responded, surprised by the question.

"Good," she replied before turning around and going back to help her father take care of the animals.

"Her mother died soon after Cleena was born," Angus informed Zebedee, guessing that he would be wondering about it.

As Zebedee walked back to London, he couldn't stop thinking about Cleena. He even slapped himself once, only to be laughed at by some children playing nearby.

"Were you trying to kill an insect on your face?" one of them asked him and laughed again.

"No…maybe," Zebedee replied, embarrassed.

After arriving in London, Zebedee headed towards his parents' house. He forgot he had his own house until he reached his parents door. Since he was there, he thought he may as well greet his parents.

He heard serious sounding voices coming from inside the house. He assumed it was a scolding of Hilda or Leofric for doing something wrong.

He knocked on the door.

Jacobus opened the door and said, "Hello Zebedee, I'm glad you came here."

After Zebedee stepped inside he was surprised by how many people were gathered inside and at how happy they all were. John, Simon, Priscilla, Hilda, Leofric, Hreodbeorht's parents and their children, Clement's parents and their children, Samson's widow Esther and her three children, Alta, and

Jacobus were all inside. Hreodbeorht had four younger siblings and Clement had five. Zebedee had never seen so many people inside his parents' house at the same time, twenty-six, including himself.

"Hello, Zebedee," everyone said more or less simultaneously.

"Now we know a little more about how the Eastern and Western churches have deviated from the Bible," Jacobus informed Zebedee. "And John isn't the only student of the Bible who thinks so."

"Oh," Zebedee replied, curious. "Please continue."

"I went to a priest, weeping, and asked him to pray with me for Samson's soul," Esther began. "I informed him that Samson hadn't confessed his sins to a priest in years. Samson said he had repented and asked God for forgiveness for his sins; he didn't see the need to confess to a priest, nor did he believe a priest could forgive our sins or convey God's forgiveness. After I narrated this to the priest, he said, 'Don't worry. He believed in the Lord Jesus, right? So he is in Heaven now.'

"'But he didn't go to confession or perform any penance,' I replied."

"Then he said, 'That doesn't matter. The Bible says that if you believe in Jesus, who took the full punishment for our sins and forgives us, you will be saved. You don't need to confess your sins to a priest; it does nothing. Samson was correct. Please don't tell anyone I told you this.'"

Esther continued, "I was baffled and protested, 'but that is not what the Church teaches. Please don't lie to comfort me. It sounds too good to be true.'"

"'I'm not lying,' he replied."

"The same thing happened to me when I went to the same priest to ask him to pray for Hreodbeorht's soul, because Hreodbeorht hadn't been to confession for months," said Abigail. "I was next in line behind Esther."

"So that means salvation is a guarantee?" Zebedee asked with amazement. "And we don't need to confess our sins to priests or anyone apart from the Lord?"

"Yes," responded Jacobus and Simon simultaneously. "Exactly."

"If Jacobus wasn't an eyewitness to the miracles at York, I wouldn't believe any of this," Alta stated and laughed nervously.

"John, please explain to us which teachings of the Church are correct and which are not," Priscilla pleaded.

"Many things the Roman churches teach about God are correct," John explained. "There is only one true God. He is one Being, yet three distinct Persons: Father, Son, and Holy Spirit. Jesus Christ is God the Son. He took on human flesh about one thousand years ago without ceasing to be God Almighty. He was born of a virgin named Mary. He lived a sinless life and died on a cross for the sins of the whole world. He rose from the dead after three days and ascended back to Heaven forty days later. He is now at the right hand of God the Father. He will come again, this time in all His glory, and establish His kingdom on the Earth. Those who believe in Him will be resurrected with immortal, glorified bodies that are like His body. Believers who are alive till His second coming will be caught up to meet Him in the air and their bodies will be transformed into immortal glorified bodies as well, but without their mortal bodies dying, as mentioned in Paul's First Letter to the Corinthians and his First Letter to the Thessalonians.

"Apart from all these truths, the Bible also teaches that we will reign with Him for a thousand years after His return. After which Heaven and Earth will be destroyed and the rest of the dead will be resurrected and judged by Him. Then those who believed in Him will live with Him forever in the new Heaven and the new Earth as written near the end of the Book of Revelation."

Everyone apart from John looked at each other in confusion. They never heard about the millennial reign of Christ. They were told that the earth would be destroyed at the Second Advent, and then immediately after that all the dead would be raised together and be judged at the final judgement.

John continued, "We are saved by God's grace alone, through faith in Christ alone, and cannot be saved by works, as Paul stated in his Letter to the Ephesians, because our good works don't nullify our sins," John continued. "This is also clear from many Scripture passages that faith is what God asks for us to live as His children. If we truly have faith in Christ we will want to please Him. God alone can forgive sins. The apostles did not have the authority to forgive sins and neither do clergymen today. By the way, the practice of confessing one's sins to clergymen has been changing over the centuries in the Roman churches."

"Wait, what about baptism?" Simon asked John.

"Yes," said Alta. "Doesn't one need to be baptized to be saved? Doesn't baptism cleanse us of all our past sins and get rid of original sin?"

"No, baptism does not save us," John replied. "Baptism does not cleanse us of our sins or our sinful nature. The Apostle Paul refers to our sinful nature as the flesh. What does that tell you? Baptism just symbolizes what has already transpired in our hearts. Only a saved person should be baptized. In baptism, the believer being baptized is telling the world publicly that he is identifying with Christ in His death and in His Resurrection. By the way, baptism is supposed to be by full immersion, not by sprinkling, as it symbolizes death and resurrection as mentioned in the Book of Romans."

"So the purpose of being baptized is to declare to the world that we are Christians?" Priscilla asked.

"Yes," John replied. "You are right. By being baptized, a believer is affirming the fact that they have been buried with Christ and have risen to new life with Him."

"Wait a minute, that means none of us has been truly baptized!" Esther exclaimed.

"That is correct," responded John. "We need to be baptized by a believer who has truly been baptized. It would be a wonderful experience to do it with the full knowledge of what it means."

"What?" Thomas and Zebedee exclaimed in shock.

"How are we supposed to find someone who has truly been baptized?" Osbeorn voiced everyone's thoughts.

"I don't know," replied John, quietly. "We will need to pray and ask God to show us what to do."

"Yes," Priscilla agreed. "We definitely need to ask the Lord to show us what to do,"

"So how does one become a member of the Church, the body of Christ, if not by being baptized?" Simon asked John.

"Just by believing in Him with all your heart and mind," John answered. "Neither the Western Roman Church nor the Eastern Roman Church is the true Church. They are just manmade establishments. The true Church is composed of all true believers in Heaven and on Earth."

"The Capital of the Eastern Church is Constantinople, not Rome," Simon said.

"When the Roman Empire split into the Eastern Roman Empire and the Western Roman Empire, Rome was the Capital of the Western Roman Empire and Constantinople became the capital of the Eastern Roman Empire," John replied.

"Oh," Simon laughed. "I see. That's why you called it the Eastern Roman Church. That makes sense."

"And about communion," John announced. "The bread and wine just symbolize Christ's body and blood. They do not actually become His body and blood, and they are not a sacrifice. Jesus died once for all, so His body and blood are not sacrificed every time we partake in the Lord's table. And communion does not save us or impart any special grace to us, but it gives us an opportunity to examine ourselves and reconcile with God before partaking of it, as taught in Paul's First Letter to the Corinthians."

"So if we shouldn't receive communion in St. Peter's Cathedral, Westminster, should we attend church there at all?" Zebedee asked John. "Don't we have to go to church and partake in communion as Christians?"

"I think we should keep going to St. Peter's Cathedral, Westminster, and receiving communion there," John answered. "I think it is fine as long as we remember that the bread and the wine are just symbols of our Lord's body and blood. Besides, what alternative do we have?"

"Why are my prayer never answered when I pray to saints?" Zebedee questioned John.

"That's right," said John. "How could I forget? We ought to pray to God alone. And Mary was not a perpetual virgin, nor was she sinless. Although she was a virgin when she gave birth to Jesus, she and Joseph had several children together after that; at least four sons and two or more daughters as recorded in the Gospels of Matthew and Mark. Mary did die a normal death like every other believer, but her body was not assumed into Heaven together with her soul and spirit when she died. Mary is not the Mother of God. Mary was merely an instrument to carry Jesus, the eternal God, who took on flesh. And of course Mary and Joseph took care of Jesus when He was a child, all because He let them do it. Do you remember Jesus asking Mary and Joseph, 'Did you not know that I must be about My Father's business?' in the Gospel of Luke when He was twelve years old? Yet He went with them and stayed with them till He began His ministry. Since all human relationships end with death, Mary stopped being Jesus' mother when He died on the cross."

Upon hearing these statements about Mary, their jaws dropped in astonishment.

"So that means Mary is not the Queen of Heaven, right?" Zebedee queried.

"That is correct." John answered. "Calling her things like the Mother of God, or the Queen of Heaven or anything else, is blasphemy against God. There is absolutely no Scriptural evidence whatsoever for these beliefs. I have repented and asked the Lord to forgive me for calling Mary 'queen', and for trusting in the other false practices of the Roman churches! You all should, too."

"Both the Western and the Eastern Roman churches are clearly wrong, but which is more correct on the teachings they disagree on?" Zebedee asked John.

"Overall, I'm not sure," John replied. "God has revealed Himself as Father, Son, and Holy Spirit. But they are needlessly arguing about the relationship within the Holy Trinity, which we cannot possibly comprehend. They should be more concerned about making the Word of God available to people and hold their services in the local language. They should not interpose the saints, angels, and themselves as intermediaries between the laity and God."

That night Zebedee wondered what would have happened if he had confessed his sin of pursuing fleeing Norwegians invaders to a priest. Zebedee imagined the priest saying, 'I don't absolve you because that was not a sin,' and sighed.

CHAPTER 6

BUDDING FEELINGS AND A WEDDING

The next evening, after Dermont, Cleena, and the ceorls who worked on Zebedee's farm were done for the day, Cleena approached Zebedee and said, "I have always loved horses; I love taking care of your horses, but I was never allowed to ride them. Will you please teach me how to ride a horse?"

"Umm, sure," Zebedee responded, gladly.

Then he reminded himself to guard his heart.

"We will start an hour after dinner," he continued.

"Which horse would you like to ride first?" he asked Cleena when they entered his stable after dinner. "The black one or the red one?"

"The chestnut mare," she replied.

"Chestnut mare…?" he muttered to himself, and then said, "Wait, aren't chestnut mares known to have quite a temper? I have heard some people say that they do, although some disagree."

"I and my father take care of them, so I don't think either will hurt me," she replied, "but I feel closer to the chestnut mare than I do to the black stallion."

The first thing Zebedee taught Cleena was how to mount and dismount. He had to help her up and down initially. Then he taught her how to give the horse commands, how to direct it to start walking, go faster, slow down, turn, and stop. Then they went for a ride around his farm. She rode on the chestnut mare and he rode on the black stallion.

"So, does this mean I can ride a horse now?" she asked him.

"Yes," he answered.

"That's great," she exclaimed. "Good night, Zebedee."

"Good night," Zebedee replied.

"I have been to the city many times, but I haven't seen much of it," Cleena told Zebedee the next morning. "Will you please give me a tour this evening?"

"Yes," he responded.

"Thank you," she said with a charming smile. "I'm too tired from the horse ride yesterday evening to ride a horse this evening. May we please go on your horse?"

"Alright," he said.

"It will be dark before you start to head back if you leave after dinner," said Dermont, who was close by. "Maybe you should leave right after the midday meal."

"Good idea," Zebedee said.

"Indeed," Cleena said, stifling a laugh.

I'm sure she will cherish the extra holiday, Zebedee mused, amused.

"Would you like to see the marketplace first?" he asked her as they entered the city.

"No, let's go there last," she chirped as sweetly as a bird. "It is in the middle of the city, and that is where I usually go when I come here anyway. Let's go along the inside of the city wall first."

The thrall on a horse received a lot of glances with raised eyebrows.

"Well, that was boring," Cleena exclaimed as they finally headed toward the marketplace. "It was mostly just houses and the city wall. I don't know what was worse."

Zebedee laughed.

"Why didn't you tell me it would be so boring?" she demanded. "Why didn't you tell me I would just see a lot of houses... Although a few were unique."

"How could the wall be boring?" he asked.

"What?" she exclaimed. "Men are so strange and boring."

The market place was bustling.

Zebedee noticed Cleena eyeing some scarves.

"Would you like one?" Zebedee asked her.

"Oh, um, yes please," Cleena replied.

Zebedee knew that she intentionally did not ask for an expensive scarf.

Zebedee and Cleena were so engaged in their conversation that neither noticed Eva watching them.

The next day onwards, Zebedee got busy with the preparations for Jacobus' wedding.

Friday, October 27, 1066, was a surprisingly warm and sunny day for the time of year.

Earlier that week Zebedee and his family heard rumors that Duke William was conquering and suppressing opposition in other parts of Engla Land, and that he probably would not come to London until he had conquered the rest of Engla Land and quelled all resistance against him.

But that was not as important to them this day, the day Jacobus was to marry the love of his life.

Zebedee couldn't help day dreaming about Cleena becoming a Christian and marrying him. He recalled their most delightful conversations and how happy he was when she was sitting behind him on the horse and holding onto him. As he suddenly became aware of the hustle and bustle of the wedding around him, he brought his attention back to the celebration of Jacobus' big day.

It goes without saying that Jacobus was wearing his finest clothes and Alta was dressed in a gown of emerald, green with a gold-flecked veil. The wedding ceremony took place just outside the main doors of St. Peter's Cathedral, Westminster. Both of them shook a little, with nervousness and excitement, as they exchanged vows and wedding rings. After the marriage contract was finalized, everyone who attended the wedding ceremony went inside the church for Mass.

"Why are my prayers never answered when I pray through saints?" Zebedee asked the priest after the Mass. "When I pray to God He sometimes grants my requests, but not when I pray through saints. It has always been like this as far as I can remember. I realized God was trying to tell me something."

"I suppose the petitions you make to the saints aren't God's will," the priest replied. "Don't stop venerating saints; they intercede for us before the throne of God, and He is so powerful and holy. How do you expect a sinner such as yourself to go before His throne directly?"

"By His mercy and grace," replied Zebedee.

"By the blood of His Son, Jesus Christ, which cleanses us from all sin," added John, who overheard the conversation and came up closer to Zebedee.

"What are you implying, John?" the priest queried. "That we can confidently pray to God directly every time and that we don't need to ask the saints in Heaven for help?"

John responded by quoting part of the passage corresponding to Hebrews 4:16 from the Latin Vulgate, "Adeamus ergo cum fiducia ad thronum gratiæ. Let us therefore come boldly to the throne of grace."

"What?" asked the priest, addled.

"That is written in the Book of Hebrews," John replied. "So you see, confidence in directly approaching God has surely been made available to us."

"There is a book in the Bible titled Hebrews?" the priest asked. "Anyways, we are not living in the Old Testament times anymore. It doesn't matter what the Hebrews believed over one thousand years ago."

"It is in the New Testament," responded John, not very surprised by the priest's lack of knowledge, because he knew that most monks in the monastery read the Bible without paying attention to the context and that the priests usually did not spend as much time reading the Bible due to their many priestly duties like celebrating the Eucharist, conducting marriages, baptisms, and funerals[10].

"What? Really?" the astonished priest asked. "Yes, now I remember, the Book of Hebrews. Well that is why you must be careful about how you interpret the Scriptures; they are very difficult to understand. If your interpretation contradicts the Church's teachings, you can be sure that you are wrong."

"Actually," responded John, laughing at the priest's ignorance. "I think it is the other way around. Since the Western and Eastern Roman churches' teachings so clearly contradict simple and straightforward portions of Scripture, we can be sure that these churches are wrong."

"Heretic!" yelled the priest. "I never thought you would become a heretic John! Do you really think that all the Christians before us were wrong and that you alone are right? How could they all have been wrong? Do you think you can understand the Bible better than any of us and any of them?"

"Why don't you read the Bible and Church history for yourself and ask me if you still have any more questions," John answered. "The Church has been gradually departing from what the Bible teaches."

"Fine, I'll read them," the priest replied. "What in the world is your abbot teaching you?"

After the Mass, Jacobus hosted a feast behind his house. Everyone was seated around two long tables. He'd hired professional cooks to prepare all the dishes.

John was contemplating what gift to give Jacobus and Alta at their wedding. He obviously could not afford to give them any material gifts. He decided to give them the honor of sponsoring a Bible translation into Englisć.

During the feast John asked Jacobus, "I know I am asking a lot, but I really want to show you all what the Bible says. Can you buy three large codices and a dozen quill pens for me? And a lot of ink as well?"

"I'm sorry, John, I cannot afford that," Jacobus said.

"I understand," John sighed. "How about one large codex, four pens, and four inkwells filled with ink, then?"

"I…I will need to speak with Alta about it," replied Jacobus nervously.

"Alright," John sighed and gave a faint smile.

"Talk to me about what?" asked Alta, coming to stand beside them.

"John was wondering if we could buy a large codex, a few quill pens, and some ink for him," responded Jacobus.

"What?" asked a shocked Alta.

"You all need to read the Bible for yourselves," John explained. "I want to translate at least the New Testament into Englisċ for you all to read."

"We are not that wealthy, John," scolded Alta. "We are a newly married couple. Are you crazy?"

"Never mind," John replied. "I will ask Thomas."

John walked over to Thomas, who was sitting beside Abigail at one of the tables, and asked, "Thomas, may I please speak with you privately for a moment?"

"Surely, my friend," replied Thomas.

John then led Thomas some distance from the rest.

"I want to translate the Scripture into Englisċ," John began. "I want you all to read what the Bible says. Can…"

"Sounds great," replied Thomas.

"Can you please buy three large codices, a dozen quill pens, and a dozen large inkwells filled with ink for me?" John asked.

"I'm sorry, John," Thomas responded. "I have been saving up to buy a house, a small farm, and some animals for Clement. His mother and I would like him to move out as soon as possible, and that is what he wants as well. It is getting a little crowded in our house. Why don't you just tell us what the Bible says? We believe you."

John stopped, his jaw half way down, as Thomas gave him a pat on the back and began to return to sit with his wife.

"Wait…" called John. "How about just one?"

"What?" Thomas asked, turning around.

"How about just one codex, four quill pens, and four inkwells?" John pleaded. "One large codex should be more than enough for the entire New Testament."

"I'm sorry, John," Thomas replied. "I can't afford that either right now."

CHAPTER 7

THE GROWING FAMILY OF BELIEVERS

On Saturday, November 4, 1066, just as Zebedee left his house, he saw John walking towards it.

"Good morning, John," Zebedee shouted joyfully.

"Good morning, Zebedee," he replied.

"What brings you here so early?" Zebedee asked.

"I think you should free your thralls," John told him.

Zebedee chuckled nervously for a brief moment. He was not sure if John was serious or just joking.

"Seriously," John said, aware of Zebedee's uncertainty.

"Does the Bible say we shouldn't have thralls?" Zebedee asked. "I know that many places, like Normandy, no longer have thralls, but why is that?"

"While the Bible doesn't say that it is wrong to have thralls, it does make it clear that we should treat them like our brothers and sisters, just like our Lord and Master Jesus Christ treats us, His thralls, like His brothers and sisters," John replied, and then began to recite part of Ephesians 6:9. Here, Paul is telling us we are all servants of Christ. We must treat those who serve us as Christ treats us.

"Well," Zebedee answered. "My thralls aren't Christians, and I don't mistreat them at all."

"Well then," John answered. "If she isn't a believer, make sure you don't fall for her."

Zebedee's face became warm as it turned red.

"I know," Zebedee said, and sighed, after calming down. "I keep hoping Cleena becomes a Christian. Wait, but what if a thrall lies about becoming a Christian so that their owner frees them?"

"That is one reason I believe Christians should let all their thralls go free," John responded. "I think, that is one reason many Christians have been discouraging the practice of owning thralls for centuries. The more important reason of course, is that many people seriously mistreat their thralls. Thralls receive very little from their owners and cannot own their own land, and unless they are freed, their children will also be thralls. There is no guarantee that their children's future owners won't mistreat them. Would you do that to your brothers?"

"If I let them go I may never see her again," Zebedee exclaimed with clear disappointment.

"Oh, it looks like you have fallen for her already," John replied. "Let them go free and hire them as ceorls if they are willing. It is illegal for a free person to marry a thrall anyway, but remember, even if you are in love with her, you can't marry her if she doesn't love our Lord."

"Oh, I did not know it was illegal," Zebedee muttered.

"What was that?" asked John.

"Nothing," Zebedee replied. "Don't worry, I will free them as soon as possible."

"Good to hear," replied John. "I'll go tell the rest."

Zebedee knew marriage between different social classes was strongly discouraged, but he did not know it was illegal for a free person to marry a thrall.

How unfair, Zebedee thought to himself as he walked over to Dermont and Cleena.

Then he realized the reason for the rule was not to maintain the wealth of those who are free but to protect thralls from forced or abusive marriages. If someone wanted to marry their thrall, what was stopping them from freeing them first? And if you wanted to marry someone else's thrall you could try to purchase their thrall from them and then free them.

I don't want to force Cleena to marry me anyway, Zebedee thought to himself. *I would never do that. And I can afford to hire them as ceorls. So I have no reason to not free her and Dermont.*

"Hello Cleena," Zebedee said when he saw her feeding the horses. "Can you please take me to your father? I need to speak with the two of you."

"Oh, all right," she replied, trying not to show her nervousness.

"Father, Zebedee would like to speak with us about something," Cleena said to her father when she found him trying to gather the pigs together.

"Just give me a minute... actually... can you please help me gather the pigs?" Dermont responded.

"Yes," she replied.

Zebedee decided to help too.

"I am going to free the two of you," Zebedee informed them.

"What?" they asked simultaneously.

Zebedee had never seen them so astonished before.

Zebedee, Jacobus, Simon, Priscilla, Esther, Thomas, Abigail, Osbeorn, and Sarah legally freed their thralls that very day after signing the necessary documents in front of witnesses.

The next day at church, what the priest read from Matthew 6:19-21 really struck Zebedee.

In the passage Jesus was telling His followers to not store up treasures on earth, but store treasures in heaven, where they cannot disintegrate or be stolen. *What is it that you want me to do, Lord?* Zebedee asked the Lord.

That night in his dream he saw Dermont and Cleena's small hut behind his house, then he saw their few cheap clothes and all his own clothes in his wardrobe. He also saw his land and animals, and finally, in his dream, he clearly recalled John asking Jacobus and then Thomas to buy him three large codices, some quill pens, and some ink. He knew this dream was from God.

He felt the Lord impress on his heart to sell his land and his animals to buy all the materials John wanted for his translation work, and to give the rest of the money to the poor.

Thoughts of *Why me?* entered Zebedee's mind. *Wait, what am I thinking? This was a great privilege that my Lord has given me to serve Him and help others, and also, maybe this will make Cleena fall in love with me.*

The next morning, he visited John in the monastery and told him what the Lord had asked him to do.

John was overcome with joy and hugged his youngest brother.

"Zebedee, once you read the Bible, you will see that the Word of the Lord is more precious than gold and sweeter than honey," he told him. "It is worth selling all that you have to read the Bible. You don't have a wife and children to take care of, so you don't need your riches. Why don't you join the monastery too? I will finish studying Koine Greek around the end of this year and then begin translating the New Testament from Koine Greek into Englisċ around the beginning of next year. I think it will take me at least ten years to translate the entire Bible into Englisċ by myself, but if you study Latin for another year, you can begin translating the Old Testament in Englisċ from the Latin Vulgate, since that is the only language we have the Old Testament in at Westminster Abbey. Together we can complete translating the entire Bible sooner, and of course you can also see what the Scriptures really teach, before the Englisċ translation is complete."

"What?" Zebedee exclaimed. "Who said I don't want to get married? God did not tell me to become a monk."

"All right, I apologize," John replied softly.

"Can you help me sell my land and animals?" Zebedee asked.

"Oh, I think it would be better if you asked Mother and Father to help you with that," he answered.

So Zebedee went to his parents' house and told them about his dream.

"What?" exclaimed Priscilla.

"Are you a fool?" Simon asked Zebedee. "It was just a dream. I get those all the time."

"We are not living in the times of the Bible," Priscilla said. "I don't think God actually spoke to you, I think you just dreamt that He did."

"Why do you want to become a ceorl?" Simon asked. "You will be the laughingstock of London."

Zebedee was so angry that he walked out of their house without saying anything.

"Zebedee, wait," Priscilla pleaded.

"Son, stop," Simon called out to him. "Use your brain. What you are saying does not make any sense."

"Yes, it does, Father," Zebedee shouted.

He went to John and told him what happened.

"Let's ask Thomas if he is interested in buying your property," John said. "He wanted to buy land and animals for Clement anyway, I just hope he hasn't done so already. And don't worry, if God wants us to do something, He will give us the means to do so."

Upon inquiring, they discovered that Thomas had already bought a house, some land, and some animals for Clement. Thomas was also too busy to help them sell Zebedee's property.

"Now what do we do?" said Zebedee.

"Why don't we go ask Osbeorn?" John suggested.

Off they went to Osbeorn's house and knocked on the door. After what seemed like ages to Zebedee and John, Osbeorn opened the door.

"Hello, Osbeorn," Zebedee greeted him. "We have a favor to ask."

"What is it, Zebedee?" he inquired.

"I need to sell my land and my animals…" Zebedee began.

"Huh?" Osbeorn asked, addled.

"Can you please help me sell them at a fair price?" Zebedee finished.

"Why do you want to sell them, Zebedee?" he asked. "That would make you a ceorl. What do you need all that money for? Are you moving to a different city…or country?"

"No," Zebedee replied. "God told me to sell them and buy somethings for John and give the rest to the poor."

"Huh? All right, I will help you," Osbeorn replied. "What do you need to buy, John?"

"Three large codices, some quill pens, and a lot of ink," John responded. "Don't tell anyone: I want to translate the Bible into Englisċ so that we can read it for ourselves."

"Oh my," exclaimed Osbeorn, "that sounds great. I will buy Zebedee's land and animals."

Osbeorn bought Zebedee's land and animals the next day after taking a loan for the purchase. He also helped John and Zebedee to buy the three large codices and all the necessary quill pens and ink. They carried one codex each as they were rather bulky and heavy.

"Now onto the challenging part," John exclaimed in a voice infused with suspense, as they walked toward the monastery.

It was clear he wanted them to ask him what the difficulty was. Osbeorn and Zebedee glanced at each other, amused. They decided not to humor him. They knew that he would continue anyway.

"Now we have to transport all these items to my room in the monastery without raising any suspicions, or better yet, without even getting noticed," John went on.

"And how are we supposed to do that?" Osbeorn questioned.

"Don't worry, just walk in," said a voice from above.

Zebedee, John, and Osbeorn were astounded, more so by God speaking to them in this way, than by what He told them to do. They obeyed. No one in the monastery paid attention to them as they entered, walked across the halls, up the stairs, and finally into John's room.

"What just happened?" Osbeorn asked ecstatically, after they all entered John's room and John closed the door behind them.

"I don't know what He did exactly, but the Lord helped us," John responded.

They couldn't tell if God put it into the hearts of the other monks to not pay any attention to them, or whether He made it so that they could neither see nor hear them.

"Thank You, Lord," John prayed out loud.

Thank You Lord Jesus, Zebedee prayed in his heart.

"God is good," exclaimed Osbeorn.

John hid the codices, inkwells, and quill pens under his bed, then escorted Zebedee and Osbeorn out of the monastery. Once again, no one stopped or questioned them.

"Thank you again, Osbeorn," Zebedee said before they all parted ways.

"You are most welcome," Osbeorn replied. "I look forward to reading the Bible for myself."

That night there was a powerful storm.

The next morning, a loud crash awoke Zebedee. He looked around his house frantically, supposing a thief had broken in. He then realized that the sound came from outside the house. He picked up his large sword and large shield and ran outside barefoot, still wearing his night clothes. He hadn't gone a few paces before he heard a young woman crying. Although he had never heard her cry before, he knew it had to be Cleena, as Dermont and Cleena's hut was the only house close by. He ran to the back of his house, worried. He was aghast at what he saw, but he was relieved that neither Cleena nor Dermont was hurt.

Dermont and Cleena were standing beside a pile of rubble which Zebedee knew used to be their hut. Cleena was crying and Dermont was hugging her.

Zebedee wondered whether he should put his sword and shield away and return without them, or whether he should talk to them right away. He decided the latter and walked over to them.

"Our hut was creaking all night during the storm," Dermont told Zebedee quietly, before Zebedee asked or said anything. "Our hut collapsed right after we stepped out this morning."

"Thank God it didn't collapse when you two were inside," Zebedee said.

"Who sent the storm?" asked Dermont, bitterly.

Zebedee was taken aback.

"I…I think He wants me to get a bigger house built for the two of you," Zebedee said.

"What?" asked Dermont.

Cleena stopped crying, turned to Zebedee, and wiped away her tears, to Zebedee's delight.

"That's right," Zebedee said. "I will look for some builders to construct a bigger house for you."

"Can you afford that?" questioned Dermont.

"Yes," Zebedee answered. "I just sold my land and my animals to a friend yesterday. You two no longer work for me."

"What?" they both gasped.

"God told me to sell them, to buy some things for one of my brothers, and to give the rest to the poor," Zebedee explained.

Their jaws dropped even further.

When all the other ceorls who worked on the farm which used to be Zebedee's arrived for work that day, he informed them that he had sold his land and animals to Osbeorn, who would be their new employer. He also told them that he was going to give the silver shillings he was paid to all of them, after paying the builders of Dermont's and Cleena's new house. Their reaction was similar to Dermont's and Cleena's.

That afternoon, Osbeorn came to look at his new property and meet those who worked on it. Simon and Priscilla came along with him.

"You know Zebedee," Priscilla began, after Zebedee had introduced Osbeorn to all the ceorls on the farm. "Your father and I miss you and Jacobus very much. Both of you left on the same day, and we haven't gotten used to it yet. Why don't you come back home and donate your house to Dermont and Cleena?"

"Huh, what?" Zebedee blurted out.

Not my house too, he thought to himself.

He immediately felt ashamed of himself.

"It will take a while for a new house to be built, son," Simon reasoned, seeing Zebedee's displeasure. "Where will they stay till then?"

Zebedee knew in his heart that they were right and he felt that God wanted him to do this too.

Zebedee sighed, and then got himself to cheer up before saying, "You are right."

"Really?" asked Dermont and Cleena simultaneously.

"Yes," Zebedee answered.

Cleena strode towards Zebedee and hugged him. Dermont followed suit and hugged both of them just as Cleena was letting go, eliciting giggles from Cleena and Zebedee.

Zebedee distributed all his silver shillings equally among all the ceorls who used to work for him. They were very grateful.

Lord, may they all see the truth about salvation, Zebedee prayed.

After moving back home with his parents, he was required to work on their farm again, but what he missed the most was Cleena. He often daydreamed about talking to her and ruminated on their amiable little conversations. He decided to visit her and Dermont that Saturday.

There was a knock on the door of Simon and Priscilla's house that Saturday morning.

"Who is it?" Priscilla asked.

"It's me, Osbeorn," came a familiar voice.

"Zebedee, can you please open the door," Priscilla said to Zebedee, who was at that very moment ready to go out to visit Cleena and Dermont.

"Yes," Zebedee said as he strode toward the door.

When he had opened it, he saw Osbeorn, who was forcing a smile.

"Good morning, Zebedee," he struggled to sound cheerful. "Is your father home?"

"Yes," Zebedee replied. "I'll go get him. I mean…please come in."

"Good morning, Osbeorn," Simon came to stand beside Zebedee the next second. "Please come in."

"Thank you," Osbeorn said, and entered the house. "I'm sorry. I shouldn't have come so early. I haven't been able to get much sleep since Hreodbeorht's death. I needed a distraction. So I was hoping you could join me on a hunt."

"Oh, most assuredly," Simon replied. "Oh wait, let me check with my wife first."

"Go ahead, dear," Priscilla replied.

"Thanks, honey," Simon responded.

"Why don't you join us too, Zebedee?" Osbeorn asked Zebedee.

"Me?" Zebedee gasped. "But…"

Osbeorn laughed, and then said, "Don't worry, lad, we will take extra precautions. I'm sure we will find something for you to do."

"But I…" Zebedee began.

Not only was he terrible at hunting, but he also wanted to spend time with Cleena that day. He realized, however, that Osbeorn wanted him to come because he missed Hreodbeorht.

"Right, surely," he replied, feigning cheer, as he wondered if the Lord was stopping him as Cleena was not a Christian.

All three of them enjoyed that hunt. There were no hunting mishaps. Zebedee improved his archery, gutting, skinning, and butchering skills.

The following day, Sunday, November 12, the Normans had still not marched into London. The city and local troops continued to remain on high alert, expecting the imminent attack.

Dermont and Cleena finally agreed to come to church with Zebedee that day. He was overjoyed.

If Cleena becomes a Christian I could marry her, he thought to himself.

Then he remembered on the way to church that he should be more concerned about their souls than about these carnal things.

"I want to know more about Jesus," Cleena said to him after the church service. "Should I ask the priest to tell me more?"

"I would like to know too," said Dermont, who was standing close by. "I believe that your God is the only true God."

Zebedee was surprised, as the service was conducted in Latin, and it dawned on him that the very fact they had come to church was because God was already convicting them.

"Umm, you may not want to ask the priest," Zebedee began, and looked at his parents briefly before looking back at Cleena and Dermont and continuing, "We will answer all your questions to the best of our ability at my parents' house."

"Why shouldn't we ask the priest?" Cleena asked, clearly confused.

"Wouldn't he know better?" queried Dermont, who was also puzzled.

"Actually, he might not, and priests are quite busy," Zebedee answered, keeping himself from letting out a small chuckle.

"I think you should call on John, just in case," Priscilla said to Zebedee as she came to stand beside him.

"Alright," Zebedee replied to his mother. "I…I will go and ask him, but his abbot may not allow him to leave on a Sunday."

"Why don't you come to our house while we wait for John," Simon said to Cleena and Dermont.

"Alright, thank you," they replied together, as Zebedee hurried off to the abbey.

"Of course I can help teach them today," replied John when Zebedee asked him. "I'll get permission to visit my family from the abbot. Let's go, little brother."

Dermont, Cleena, and the same group of twenty-six people who had previously gathered at Simon and Priscilla's house gathered there once again. John explained the Gospel and the basic tenets of the Christian faith to Cleena and Dermont in front of them all.

"My goodness," exclaimed Cleena. "All that sounds wonderful."

"Thank you very much for explaining all that," said Dermont. "But what do we need to do now?"

"Believe in the Lord Jesus Christ with all your heart and mind, and you will be saved from sin and its punishment," responded John. "Repent of your sins and ask Him to forgive you of your sins. Surrender your life to Him. Accept Him as your only Lord and Savior. Once you do, the Holy Spirit will come and dwell in you and make you a new creation. He will empower you to live for Him."

"O God forgive me!" Dermont prayed out loud, crying. "I have been so stubborn for so long. I give myself to You now."

"Thank you Lord Jesus for dying for me!" prayed Cleena. "Please forgive me of all my sins. I accept You as my Lord and Savior."

Tears of joy streamed down the faces of every adult gathered there. They all hugged Dermont and Cleena. The group of twenty-six had become the group of twenty-eight.

"Welcome into the family of God," John said to them. "You are now His children."

John also explained many of the differences between what the Roman churches taught and what the Bible teaches so that they would not be confused.

Friday of that week, Zebedee was planning on seeing Cleena at his old farm the next day. He was contemplating telling her how he felt about her and asking her to marry him.

Would I offend her by asking her to marry me? Zebedee pondered. *She is beautiful and I am ugly. Maybe I can woo her with jewelry. I can sell my sword and shield to buy some.*

It was the norm for a man to woo the woman he wanted to marry with gifts along with his proposal for her hand in marriage. He then wondered if they should live in his parent's house or Dermont's house if they did marry, but it was not God's will.

Zebedee, you shall not get married, God spoke to Zebedee. *I have given you the gift of celibacy.*

What? Zebedee exclaimed in silent shock and sorrow, tears streaming down his cheeks. *Why, O Lord? Why me?*

My child, I have a special calling for you, God answered him gently. *You won't know all the reasons till you come home, but you will know some of them soon, and you will thank Me. Remember, I only give good gifts to My children and I will work all things together for your good. Neither Cleena nor marriage will give you true joy. That is something only I can give you. Find your joy in Me. The only relationship that will make you truly happy is your relationship with Me.*

Zebedee knew what the Lord said had to be true, but he still cried for some time.

Lord, you know I love her, he prayed. *I need You to help me. Please remove my romantic love for her and help me love her as a sister.*

Maybe God is just testing me like He tested Abraham by commanding Him to offer his son Isaac, Zebedee hoped. *Maybe He wants me to stop my love for Cleena from becoming greater than my love for Him.*

Zebedee asked John what the Bible said about celibacy and asked him if it said that celibacy was a gift.

"Yes, it does," John replied before showing him the passages corresponding to Matthew 19:10-12 and 1 Corinthians 7:1-9. John had to translate a few words here and there because Zebedee was not quite fluent in Latin.

"Jesus said this does not apply to every man, but it is given to some men. Some men are celibate, or eunuchs, for the kingdom of Heaven. In Corinthians 7:1-9, Scripture says, it is good for a man not to touch a woman, or even if he has been widowed, to refrain from touching another woman, as Paul himself lived."

Zebedee still saw Cleena every Sunday, but he guarded his heart and did not let himself fall more deeply in love with her. He still spoke to her, but less often than before. A few weeks later, Zebedee realized his romantic feelings for her were finally gone and he just loved her as a sister. He then realized it was not a test.

On Sunday, December 24, as Simon, Priscilla, and Zebedee left their residence, locked the door, and headed to St. Peter's Cathedral, Westminster,

Zebedee noticed a small group of people surreptitiously leaving the crowd heading to the cathedral, then turn, and walk away on a different path.

Zebedee's first thought was that they were either rebels against William or spies working for Duke William to hunt the rebels. Upon further consideration, he thought they were probably the former because they seemed to be neglecting church. A spy would go to the church to see what the priest and laity would say about William during or after the Mass. William himself was very close to London and was wreaking havoc in some of the villages nearby.

Follow them, Zebedee, God told Zebedee. *Don't let them notice you following them. I will help you.*

"Ye...Yes Lord," Zebedee replied out loud.

"What?" Zebedee's parents asked him.

"See those people breaking away from the crowd?" Zebedee asked them and stopped walking along with the crowd so his parents would stop and look.

"Yes," they said.

"God told me to follow them," he explained.

"Oh," Priscilla responded. "Should we come with you?"

"I don't think so," he answered.

He wanted his parents to come with him but God had not told him to take them along.

"Alright," they replied.

Zebedee began to follow them as stealthily as he could. He maintained a ten to fifteen second distance between them and himself. Owing to the crisscross nature of the trek, he knew that if he maintained a greater distance he may lose them. He followed them undetected, making a lot less noise than he normally would, as they walked down quiet narrow streets and between houses.

Finally, they left all the houses behind and headed toward an old, abandoned chapel which was very close to the city wall. He had seen the chapel from the outside a few times before.

Why have I never thought about entering it before? he wondered. *That's right, I did think about it, but I thought there wouldn't be anything interesting and being so dilapidated it could fall apart any moment.*

After the group entered the chapel, he too left the row of houses and headed toward it. He casually walked toward it to avoid raising any suspicions. His heart raced as he gently opened the door.

"Greetings…" a voice began and then stopped.

The voice belonged to a man of average height who was slightly stout. He was standing, like most people in the chapel. Like in most churches, there were no benches or chairs or barrels or anything else to sit on, except for some stone benches along the walls; the elderly and disabled were sitting on them.

Everyone he could see was looking at him. Some just appeared shocked, while others seemed suspicious and nervous.

"Why are you here, friend?" asked the man who had greeted him at the door.

"I saw a small group of people leave the crowd that was headed to the cathedral I usually attend," Zebedee answered honestly. "Then God told me to follow them, so I did."

"Then welcome, brother," said the greeter at the door, joyfully. "My name is Peter."

"Hello Peter," Zebedee replied. "It is very nice to meet you. I'm Zebedee."

"It is nice to meet you too," Peter responded. "We are a gathering of true believers, true Christians."

"Whaaat?" Zebedee began, confused. "I see…"

He concluded that they knew what the Bible really taught, but it seemed like Peter was implying that those who go to other churches were not true believers. That was what surprised Zebedee the most, as he knew many true Christians who were still part of the Western Roman Church.

"Come in," said Peter, stepping beside Zebedee and placing his hand on his upper back, gently pushing him inside. "We will explain everything."

As Peter stepped behind him, Zebedee noticed that everyone's faces had lit up.

He heard the door close behind him.

"Welcome, Zebedee," they greeted him, one by one.

He was eventually brought before the old man standing at the front, who was facing everyone else.

So this is the…what are they called? Zebedee wondered what the leader of a church was called in the Bible. *John didn't tell us.*

"Welcome, brother Zebedee," he said, giving Zebedee a hug, much to his surprise. "My name is Barzillai."

"It is nice to…an honor to meet you, sir," Zebedee replied.

"Please, call me Barzillai," he responded.

"Sorry, sir…Barzillai," Zebedee replied.

"It's fine," laughed Barzillai. "Tell me, do you know your eternal destiny?"

"Excuse me? What?" Zebedee asked.

"Where you will go when you die," he explained.

"Yes," Zebedee responded. "I do know. I am going to go to Heaven when I die. I will live with my Lord Jesus Christ forever because I believe in Him."

Barzillai said, "Very good! How did you come to the knowledge of the truth?"

"My oldest brother is a monk," Zebedee answered with a little bit of pride. "He is teaching us what the Bible really says."

"Us?" asked Barzillai, clearly pleasantly surprised. "How many of your family and friends know?"

"Hmm," Zebedee responded. "I never thought to count…definitely over a dozen…let me see…twenty…no twenty-seven now,"

"Praise God," Barzillai exclaimed.

Upon hearing this, the rest of the congregation began to praise God as well. It was very different from the way the clergy and the laity praised God in other churches. Those gathered in the old chapel were truly rejoicing and praising God from their hearts, not just with their lips.

Zebedee tried to understand how they felt. He was so overwhelmed by this experience that he almost began to cry with tears of joy.

The service began with Barzillai praying aloud in Englisċ. Then they all sang beautiful songs of praise and worship in Englisċ. In the Western Roman churches, the service was conducted in Latin, regardless of how many of the laity understood Latin. Zebedee knew some Latin as most thegns learned Latin in a monastery, but most ceorls did not know more than a few words of Latin.

"The opening passage today is from near the end of the Book of Romans," Barzillai began after the songs. He then proceeded to read Romans 13:1-3.

How astonishing, thought Zebedee. *He already has an Englisċ translation of the Bible. So why did God ask me to sell my property to buy those supplies for John?*

The message, of course, was about obeying authority, except when earthly leaders made laws that contradicted God's commandments. This was very timely, as they would probably have a new monarch soon. It would be tempting to rebel against the new monarch. None of them wanted a foreign king reigning over them.

After Barzillai's sermon, there was a time of discussion.

"But what if Duke William tries to get rid of our culture and introduces the Norman culture instead?" someone protested.

"As long as obeying the king doesn't mean disobeying God, we need to obey the king," replied Barzillai. "We need to obey the king out of obedience to God."

After the discussion, everyone who wanted to pray aloud did so, one at a time.

"Now, before we partake in the bread and cup, I will read what the Apostle Paul wrote about the Lord's bread and cup in his First Letter to the Corinthians," Barzillai said.

After reading the passage corresponding to 1 Corinthians 11:23-34, he said, "Notice that Jesus said, '…do this in remembrance of Me' and 'drink it, in remembrance of Me'. Also notice that Paul wrote, 'For as often as you eat this bread and drink the cup, you proclaim the Lord's death until He comes.' What does this tell us? The bread and wine do not become the actual body and blood of our Lord Jesus Christ. They are just symbols. They do not impart any special grace unto us or save us. But of course communion is an ordinance instituted by the Lord Jesus Christ Himself and is therefore very important. Only true believers may partake in communion, and we must examine ourselves and partake in a worthy manner."

I knew John was right, Zebedee thought to himself, *but this additional independent confirmation that John is correct is very comforting.*

After the service, those in attendance met everyone who was not in their immediate families. Zebedee had a very difficult time remembering names and faces.

After everyone else had left, Zebedee stayed back to speak with Barzillai. His wife, Deborah, left too, to prepare the midday meal. Barzillai informed Zebedee about many of their teachings that differed from the teachings of the Roman churches.

"So, Zebedee, which of these surprise you?" Barzillai asked him.

"The ones that surprised me were not celebrating any holidays and not killing any human no matter what, even to defend your loved ones or your country," Zebedee replied sadly. "This means I murdered three more Norwegians than I thought I did at the Battle at Stamford Bridge."

"Three additional?" Barzillai asked.

"The late King Harold commanded us to show no mercy and his army began to pursue the invaders after they began to flee," Zebedee explained. "I and two of my friends pursed two of the fleeing invaders. One engaged me in combat, the other engaged one of my friends in combat, but my other friend shot each of them with an arrow."

"The Lord will forgive you; you just need to repent and ask Him to forgive you," Barzillai replied, putting his hand on Zebedee's shoulder.

"I know," Zebedee replied, forcing a smile.

"So, Zebedee, tell me your story," Barzillai said. "What did you feel about Christianity before hearing the true gospel and how do you feel about it now? How did you know that your oldest brother was right?"

So Zebedee told Barzillai that he, his parents, and his brothers did believe in the Lord Jesus Christ with all their hearts, even before John began teaching them what the Bible really says about things like salvation, baptism, and communion. He told him all the important details about the battle at Stamford Bridge and what happened in York days later.

"I'm surprised," exclaimed Barzillai. "And all this time I thought that no member of the Roman churches was saved, But you certainly already have a personal relationship with Jesus Christ. The Roman churches would call us heretics and kill us if they found out about this congregation, so please don't tell anyone about us, apart from those who know that the teachings of the Roman churches are straying further and further away from the Bible."

"I understand," Zebedee responded. "By the way, Barzillai, we would like to be baptized. John told us that he thinks we need to be baptized by a Christian who has truly been baptized; we have been hoping to find one and asking God to show us what to do since then."

"Of course I will baptize you," Barzillai replied. "I would love to have the privilege of baptizing all of you who have committed your lives to Christ."

"Thank you very much," Zebedee exclaimed.

"It is my pleasure," Barzillai responded. "I have never thought about what unbaptized believers who cannot find baptized believers should do. Maybe they should baptize each other? Baptism isn't a ritual, after all."

"I see," said Zebedee, with a thoughtful expression, before thanking Barzillai and leaving.

Well then, it is a good thing I forgot to wish the congregants Merry Christmas, Zebedee thought, amused, as he walked home that Christmas Eve.

When he informed the others, not including John, who was not present, about everything he discovered, they were all astonished.

"So it was a secret church, not a band of rebels," Simon exclaimed. "I never would have guessed that there existed a secret assembly in Engla Land, and right here in London."

Zebedee then went to the monastery and informed John, who did not seem very surprised.

"I knew there had to be some Bible believing Christians out there who are not part of the Roman churches," John exclaimed joyfully. "And I am not very surprised by their beliefs that surprised you, either. Although I don't think it is wrong to celebrate Christmas and Easter as yearly holidays, it is not necessary to do so. And we definitely should not observe any of the so called 'saints' days.' As for not being allowed to kill humans to defend yourself and others, I disagree with that, too, although I was wondering about that. And praise the Lord, an Englisċ translation of the Bible exists. If Barzillai agrees to lend us his manuscripts, all we need to do is make copies, which is much simpler than translating the Bible into Englisċ. Anyway, I would very much like to meet them as soon as possible. You wouldn't happen to know where Barzillai lives, would you?"

"No," Zebedee answered, "but we are all going there next Sunday and would like you to come too."

"Of course I will," replied John.

CHAPTER 8

CORONATION

Duke William and his forces marched into London the very next day. William had now conquered all of Engla Land and suppressed all opposition against himself. Eorl Edwin, Eorl Morcar, and Edgar the Ætheling were among those who opposed him, but they eventually surrendered when it was clear that their defeat was imminent.

I am surprised that William let them live, Zebedee thought to himself. *I guess he really hated the late King Harold. He wouldn't even let Harold's mother, Gytha, bury her son's body. She offered him Harold's weight in gold but he still refused and issued an order that Harold's body should be chucked into the sea, although there were some rumors that some loyal Anglo-Saxons quietly took his body and buried it somewhere. Of course, even if this were true, William and his officials wouldn't confirm it because it would be an embarrassment to him.*

"I don't believe it is a coincidence that William marches into London and wants his coronation on Christmas Day," Simon remarked. "He must be trying to convince us that God has chosen him as the next king."

"You are right, dear," Priscilla agreed.

There was a knock on Simon's and Priscilla's door shortly after they and their youngest son finished breakfast.

"I'll see who it is," Zebedee announced as he walked to the door.

"Good morning, Zebedee," Cleena greeted him after he opened the door. "Are you going to go to St. Peter's Cathedral, Westminster, to witness the coronation of William of Normandy as the new king of Engla Land?"

"Uh, yes" he answered.

"Wonderful," she exclaimed, her eyes lighting up. "Would you like to go together?"

"Yes," Zebedee responded without thinking.

The sparkle in Cleena's eyes only briefly vanished upon seeing Zebedee's confusion and uneasiness. She then boldly locked her right arm with his.

"Then let's go," she exclaimed.

"Zebedee," Priscilla shouted. "Where are your manners? Invite her in. The coronation won't start for at least a couple of hours."

Zebedee blushed and turned around to see that his parents' cheeks had turned red too.

"You are still very thin," Priscilla said to Cleena. "You haven't been eating enough. Sit down, I will get you something to eat."

"All right," Cleena laughed. "Thank you, Priscilla."

"Thank you again," exclaimed Cleena after finishing her second breakfast. "That was a treat."

"Aren't your parents going to the coronation?" Cleena questioned Zebedee as they walked toward St. Peter's Cathedral, Westminster.

"No," he answered.

"Neither is my father," she replied.

"Oh," Zebedee replied. "How come?"

"Because he doesn't care about who the new ruler will be," she responded. "How about your parents?"

"They are not happy about Engla Land being conquered," Zebedee said and laughed.

"How about you?" Cleena asked.

"It doesn't bother me much, although I miss the late King Harold," Zebedee answered. "I just want to see the coronation."

"So do I," Cleena replied.

"We still have some time; let's walk around a bit," Cleena suggested.

"Alright," Zebedee said, "but I don't think…I don't think we should walk with our arms locked together like this."

"Why?" she asked, frowning.

They both stopped walking and Cleena released Zebedee's arm.

"And why haven't you been coming to visit?" she asked, her temper briefly flaring.

She looked away from Zebedee, but he could see that her anger had turned to sorrow.

Zebedee did not know what to say.

"I love you, Zebedee," she said, quietly after turning to him again.

Zebedee was astounded by her confession. Her eyes betrayed her sadness, even though she had put on a smile. Her sorrow filled him with grief.

Lord, please help her know Your will, he prayed silently.

"I can't," Zebedee replied quietly. "God told me to stay celibate forever."

"What?" she asked with a choked voice.

"God told me to stay…" Zebedee began, facing the ground, with his eyes closed, before he felt a moderately hard slap on his left cheek.

"Well then, you shouldn't have been so nice to me," she shouted as streams rolled down her cheeks. She then broke into a sob and put her face in her hands.

Zebedee became weepy, as well, but he fought back the tears. He did not know what to say, but then decided he had to say something.

"I love you as a sister, Cleena," he finally said.

"Is that supposed to make me feel better?" she screamed. "You men are so ignorant."

She then dropped to her knees and cried even harder.

Zebedee wanted to kneel down and hug her to comfort her, but he knew that it would probably have the opposite effect, so he remained standing. He noticed people were looking at them and began fidgeting, hoping he didn't look bad.

"I think I'm going to go home," Cleena said quietly. She rose to her feet after her sobbing turned to sniffling.

"Let me…May I walk you home?" Zebedee asked.

"No," she replied. "I'll be fine. I walked here by myself."

O God, please comfort her, Zebedee prayed silently as they parted ways.

Zebedee headed to St. Peter's Cathedral, Westminster, which had been built by the late King Edward. Previously, there was only a small monastery there and the present cathedral had been completed about six years earlier. It was consecrated almost exactly a year earlier. Almost every building in Engla Land was made out of wood. This church was the only stone structure in the country. Much of Europe preferred stone structures over wooden structures by then, and King Edward did not want to be left behind in a different era. He was buried there about a week after it was consecrated. Rumor had it that one of the reasons he had it built was so he could be buried there.

On the way to St. Peter's Cathedral, Westminster, Zebedee met Jacobus and Alta. There were soldiers on every street leading to the church, one row on each side of the street. On their way there, they saw William making his way to the cathedral on horseback, riding between two lines of soldiers.

Once they arrived at the church, Zebedee tried looking for Clement but couldn't find him in the large crowd. Nearly two thousand Londoners were gathered inside, along with nearly three hundred Normans.

A Norman bishop said something in Norman. Zebedee, who had been to the coronation of the late King Harold, assumed that this Norman bishop was saying something similar, and he was correct.

"Oui! Oui! Oui!" the Normans replied.

Zebedee wondered what the name of this bishop was and if an Englisċ speaking bishop would ask the Anglo-Saxons the same thing in Englisċ.

"That is Geoffrey, the bishop of Coutances," Zebedee heard a man standing in front of him whisper to another.

"My fellow Anglo-Saxons," Ealdred, the archbishop of York, began in Englisċ. "Would you take William to be your king?"

"Yes," the Anglo-Saxons answered in one accord, to Zebedee's astonishment.

God puts rulers in their positions, so maybe I shouldn't be surprised, Zebedee concluded. *Or was it because of fear of being killed if they didn't give their consent?*

It looks like William was trying to make the Anglo-Saxons and the Normans get along, Zebedee realized. *Maybe he will be a good king after all. Wait, any smart king would try to win the loyalty of his subjects. No king wants to face insurrections. Even if he could easily crush the uprisings, he would lose subjects. What kind of king will William be? I suppose only time will tell.*

Loud cheering and rejoicing broke out among both the Anglo-Saxons and the Normans.

After a few minutes, those gathered inside the church heard some clamor coming from outside the church. Suddenly, the doors opened from the outside and smoke began to enter the cathedral. Those gathered inside watched in horror as four Norman soldiers stood before them with their swords drawn while fires were burning down some houses behind them.

"They invited us all here to massacre us!" an Anglo-Saxon woman wailed loudly.

Some Normans shouted something in their language.

All the people in the church whom Zebedee could see, apart from Jacobus and Alta, were clearly petrified and began to tremble. Most people in the church, including many who really loved the Lord, were not prepared to die at such short notice.

Almost everyone ran outside. Most of the Anglo-Saxons were trying to help put out the fires burning down theirs' and their neighbors' houses, while most of the Normans were trying to take advantage of the situation and plunder as much as they could, although, to Zebedee's astonishment, some Normans were helping the Anglo-Saxons put out the fires.

"I'm taking Alta home," Jacobus shouted to Zebedee over the tumult. "I suggest you go home too."

"I think we should stay back and help," Alta said.

"No," replied Jacobus. "You are not going anywhere near those fires. Besides, we don't know what the Normans are going to do next."

Jacobus grabbed his wife's hand and started walking away.

Alta felt elated that Jacobus loved her so much and wanted to keep her safe.

Zebedee was happy that he did not need to worry about protecting a wife as he went to help put out the fires.

With buckets and pots, people were drawing water from the River Thames to throw on the fires. Fortunately for the Anglo-Saxons, the river was close by and was not frozen that day.

I'm glad my parents' and Jacobus' houses aren't nearby, Zebedee thought to himself as he threw a bucket of water on one of the burning houses.

"Help! Please!" Zebedee heard a woman shriek and cry nearby. "My babies! Oh God, please don't take away my babies! They are all I have left!"

"Where are they?" Zebedee asked, running to her.

"In there," she said, pointing to the house in front of her. "I lost my husband already this year at the battle at Stamford Bridge. Please save my little children!"

Zebedee felt energy flow through him like never before. Without asking for permission, he took the woman's cloak, intending to give it back if it did not burn up, and ran toward the fire. He used the cloak to briefly suppress the fire at the door to the house and jumped inside. He saw a little girl and an even smaller boy in the middle of the house, sitting on the floor and crying with their faces in their hands They looked to be about seven and four years of age, respectively.

"Hello there," Zebedee said to them. "There is no need to cry. God is watching over you. Jesus loves you. Do you have any more brothers or sisters?"

They looked up at him and shook their heads as their sobbing turned to sniffling.

"Just the two of us," the little girl replied.

They began to cough because of the smoke and so did Zebedee.

As Zebedee bent down to pick them up, he heard a groaning sound coming from the roof directly above them. Then a small piece of flaming wood fell to the floor beside them. Then there was another louder groaning. Knowing what was coming next, Zebedee pushed them down and covered their bodies with his.

"Hey," they protested, right before the roof came crashing down on them.

"I see the man's body," a man shouted somewhat later, after the fire was put out while the rubble was being cleared…

"All most there, men," another man shouted, encouragingly.

This woke up Zebedee and the little children.

"Are you two all right?" Zebedee asked quietly, and stifled a groan as his body ached all over.

"Yes," the little girl replied cheerfully. "I am fine. Thank you, kind stranger. Are you all right, Harold?"

"Yes, Martha, I'm fine," her brother responded cheerfully as well. "I am glad this man showed up when he did."

Zebedee carried the children and came out when enough of the rubble was cleared.

"Thank you," Zebedee and Martha said to their rescuers, who stood still as they gaped in astonishment.

"Thank you," Harold squealed as he jumped into the arms of his mother, who had been shouting her children's names all through the ordeal.

"They're alive, they're alive," exclaimed someone in the crowd as the rest applauded. Most of the fires had been put out by this time.

"Thank you, young man," said the mother of the children.

"We would have been crushed by the roof if it wasn't for him, Mama," Martha informed her mother.

"I know, sweetie," Martha's mother replied. "I know."

"I can't believe he didn't even break a bone," laughed one of the rescuers. "It is nothing short of a miracle."

"May God bless you," Martha's mother said to Zebedee. "What is your name, kind stranger?"

"Zebedee," replied Zebedee. "What's yours?"

"Lydia," replied the woman.

"Why were they alone in the house, Lydia?" Zebedee queried.

"Since my husband died I have had to work long hours to provide for us all," she explained. "And I couldn't find anyone to watch over them today."

"What will you do now?" Zebedee asked.

"I will go to my brother," she answered. "He lives very close to London. I'm sure he and his wife will let us stay with them, even if they would prefer not to."

They all laughed.

"I may never see you three again, but you need to know something," Zebedee began.

"What is it?" Lydia asked.

"The Lord Jesus Christ is the only way to God," Zebedee told her. "He paid the full punishment for our sins on the cross. Salvation is a gift He offers to all those who turn to Him. Trust in Him with all your heart and look to Him for your every need. Christianity is not just a religion; it is a relationship with the Lord Jesus Christ."

Thank You, Lord," Zebedee prayed silently as he walked back to his parents' house. *Thank You for protecting me and those two little children. Thank You that we weren't hurt much.*"

The next morning, there was a knock on Simon's door. Zebedee and his parents were alarmed, presupposing it was one of William's troops.

I wonder what they could want now, Zebedee pondered.

"If it was a multitude of soldiers we would have heard them coming," Simon whispered as he went to get his sword and shield. Zebedee followed his lead.

"Wait," Priscilla said. "Even if it is one of William's troops, they may not be here to harm us. Don't attack."

The person outside knocked on the door again.

"Who is it?" Simon asked as he quietly approached the door with Zebedee at his heels.

"It's me, John," came the familiar voice.

The occupants of the house sighed in relief.

Simon and Zebedee sheathed their swords before Simon opened the door.

"Hello…" John began, but stopped as they all motioned him to come inside.

Simon immediately closed the door after he entered.

Priscilla and Simon hugged John before Zebedee could ask him anything, but they had the same question.

"Why did you come at this time?" Simon asked his eldest son. "It's not safe outside."

"Actually, it is safe," John replied, and chuckled. "I came to inform you about what happened yesterday, and I suppose I wanted to see you all, too."

"What happened!? What happened!?" they asked him.

"William didn't give the order for any houses to be burned or anyone to be killed," John told them.

"Yes, tell that to the people who lost their houses and their loved ones yesterday," Zebedee remarked.

"William angrily demanded that the bishops crown him king of Engla Land regardless of whether or not there was a congregation to witness it, stating he had nothing to do with the riots outside the abbey," John continued. "So the bishop of York crowned him king. After the ceremony, he angrily demanded why his guards set those houses on fire. The guards explained that they mistook the noise inside for a revolt against William. According to the custom in such situations, they set the nearby houses on fire. The actions of the Norman soldiers lead many of the Normans inside Westminster to believe that there was an uprising against William."

"That is astonishing," the rest of them replied.

"I suppose the guards were very tense and were expecting a rebellion," Zebedee said.

"Yes," Priscilla responded, nodding. "That makes sense."

The next day, the Normans began constructing a building near the middle of the city, along the northern bank of the River Thames. They were using the old Roman wall, called London Wall, as part of the structure. There was still a lot of animosity between the Normans and the Anglo-Saxons; they did not trust each other. The Anglo-Saxons looked at the construction suspiciously as they passed by.

Some asked the Normans, "What are you building?"

"A castle for the defense of London," was the response.

"Clearly King William wants the castle built to defend himself from rebels, not to defend himself from invading armies," Clement whispered to Zebedee as they passed the site.

Zebedee chuckled.

"It's not funny," whispered an annoyed Clement. "Why does he expect rebellions?"

"Maybe it is because of the fires," Zebedee answered, not realizing it was a rhetorical question with a very different implied answer.

"No, Zebedee," replied Clement. "It means he is going to be a tyrant."

CHAPTER 9

SEPERATION, NOT REFORMATION

The following Sunday, all twenty-eight believers who had been learning the true meaning of being a Christian, gathered in front of Simon's house in the morning, while most of the people in London were leaving their homes, or just about to leave, to go to their church.

Even though monks are required to worship together on Sundays, John managed to sneak out of Westminster Abbey as he knew that his duty toward God and His word superseded the rules of the monastery. Thoughts of incurring punishment and even excommunication did not deter him.

Zebedee avoided making eye contact with Cleena and Dermont because he thought they may still have acrimony towards him.

"All right, it looks like everyone is here," John said in a hushed voice. "We are going to follow Zebedee to the secret assembly."

"Lead the way, son," Simon said to Zebedee.

I thought they would all…or at least the adults… would know the way to the old chapel, thought Zebedee, who was not sure if he remembered the way very well.

They all followed Zebedee, who slowly began to walk in the direction he had the previous Sunday.

In a few minutes, when they were approaching a fork, he couldn't remember which path to take.

I guess the others don't know the way to the chapel because they don't go there on purpose, thought Zebedee and prayed silently: *Lord, please help me! I don't remember the way very well.*

"Why are you walking so slowly?" John complained. "I would like to meet them as soon as possible."

Then suddenly Zebedee remembered where to go next.

"Sorry," Zebedee replied. "I forgot which way to go, but I remember now."

Zebedee picked up the pace. As they kept walking, Zebedee was able to picture in his mind the exact path he had traversed when he followed those believers the Sunday before.

"I heard you almost died on the day of William's coronation," Cleena whispered to Zebedee, after coming up beside him. "I wish you had died."

Zebedee was shocked and dejected. He could not accept that Cleena could be so vindictive.

How could she hate me so much? he thought to himself. *I don't think she does.*

When he saw the chapel, Zebedee sighed with relief and slowed down.

"We are here," he announced, turning around.

The rest of the group cheered and began to walk past him.

"Wait," Jacobus announced. "I think Zebedee should enter the chapel first and introduce us."

Zebedee ran around them to the front and entered the chapel first.

"Good morning, Zebedee," said a man at the door.

"Good morning," replied Zebedee. "Sorry, I can't remember your name."

"Don't worry," said the man with a chuckle. "I know you have a lot of new names to remember. My name is Abraham. It is very nice to see that you brought so many of your friends and family with you."

They all quietly walked into the almost tumbledown chapel with radiant faces.

"Zebedee," rang the voice of a little girl.

"Zebedee," rang the voice of a smaller boy.

"Martha, Harold," Zebedee exclaimed with joy. He bent down as they ran towards him.

They hugged him and he returned the embrace as Lydia walked toward them.

After introducing Lydia, Martha, and Harold to those who came with him, Zebedee asked Lydia, "Is this your first time here?"

"Yes," she replied. "My brother's farm was one of those which William set on fire as he headed toward London. My brother and his family perished in the fire. I cried out to God for help. I thought I would have to sell the three of us into thralldom. I asked God to help me sell us to a benevolent person. Then we came back to the market place in London. That is when I saw Barzillai. I could tell he was a wealthy thegn. I asked him if he would buy us as thralls. He said he needed to speak to his wife and invited us to his house. Barzillai told Deborah what happened and Deborah asked us for our story. So we told them. After speaking together privately, they told me that they would rather adopt me as their daughter and my children as their grandchildren."

After saying this, Lydia covered her mouth with her left hand and began to cry.

After composing herself, she continued, "They said they had been praying for children for decades and that God hadn't given them any yet, and they were wondering if they should adopt children who have been abandoned and left in front of convents for nuns to take care of. But they decided that they should adopt me and that I can adopt other children if I want. And they told me what you told me on Christmas Day, and so much more."

"Wonderful!" Zebedee and Priscilla exclaimed simultaneously as their eyes began to water.

Priscilla hugged Lydia. She then hugged Martha and Harold and kissed their cheeks.

"What sweet children you have," she said to Lydia.

"Greetings everyone," Barzillai began when it was time for the service to begin. "I am glad to see so many new faces today. My name is Barzillai. I am of Jewish descent. My ancestors fled from Jerusalem when it was captured and destroyed by the Roman Empire in 70 AD. They fled with a complete copy of all the books of the Old Testament and most of the books of the New Testament. They were aware of exactly which books belonged to the Old Testament. About two hundred years ago some of my ancestors migrated to Engla Land with newer copies of all the books of the Bible. The next generation, who were scholars in Hebrew, Aramaic, Greek, and Englisċ, translated the entire Bible into Englisċ. They spread the true gospel of Jesus Christ in Engla Land as they did in other countries. Their numbers grew like wild fire, but the apostate Roman Church persecuted them and murdered most of them. That is why we are so few today. That Englisċ translation of the Bible was hidden, so it was not destroyed by the Roman Church, but those codices wore out due to repeated use over the centuries. These codices in front of me contain a translation with current Englisċ. There are more communities of true believers who gather in secret, not only in other countries, but also right here in Engla Land. Please don't think that we hate the members of the apostate Roman churches or anyone else; we don't. Now, let us all praise and worship our Lord together, for He is good and His mercy endures forever. He has done and will do more than we can ask or think or imagine."

Barzillai preached about forgiveness after they all finished singing. Barzillai first spoke about Christ forgiving those who crucified Him and forgiving Peter for denying he even knew Him.

"You may think, 'We cannot be so forgiving, like Jesus, who is God,' but the disciples would have also forgiven those who tortured and killed them and their loved ones."

Barzillai then spoke about Joseph forgiving his brothers and David forgiving Saul.

After the service, Barzillai spoke to the thirty-one — which included the group of twenty-eight plus Lydia, Martha, and Harold — newest members of the congregation.

"Do you want to follow the Lord Jesus Christ with all your heart, mind, and strength?" Barzillai asked after explaining basics tenets of the faith about the Holy Trinity, Jesus' death on the cross for our sins and His Resurrection, the indwelling of the Holy Spirit in believers to enable them to walk with God, and the second coming of Christ.

They all responded with either, "Yes," or "I do."

"Then you should all leave the apostate Roman Church," Barzillai announced. "It would be my pleasure to baptize those of you who do, who are above the age of eight, who have made a personal commitment to follow Christ, and who want to be baptized next Sunday after the service. We have found that most children below that age may not be able to understand the gospel and make an informed decision to follow Jesus no matter what. Of course there have been exceptions, but they are very rare, so we don't baptize children below the age of eight. I will now show you all where my house is. If you have any questions or concerns, feel free to come to my house."

"I wanted to translate the Bible into Englisċ," John said to Barzillai. "I know you have an Englisċ translation, but I want to keep a translation of the entire Bible at my parents' house, so that we can all read it anytime we want to. Would you let me come to the chapel every day to copy your translation?"

"Absolutely," replied Barzillai. "There is no need for you to remain in the monastery. By staying in the monastery, you are subjecting yourself to your abbot's authority, and therefore remain a part of the apostate Roman Church. I just hope they don't cause you too much trouble. And please remember to not mention this gathering."

"Well then, it is a good thing that I have not really started my translation work yet," said John. "It would be better to copy your translation than to translate from the Latin Vulgate. Thank you very much, Barzillai."

"It is my pleasure," Barzillai replied.

"Are you sure that neither the Western Roman Church nor the Eastern Roman Church can be reformed?" Esther asked Barzillai.

"Yes," responded Barzillai. "They will never be reformed enough to justify staying."

"He is correct," John said. "After I completed reading the entire Bible twice, I have been asking my abbot questions about my understanding from reading the Scriptures and the teachings and practices of the Roman churches, which clearly do not align, hoping that he would think about it and seek the truth, but he was just too stubborn. I was punished for asking so many questions and not just blindly accepting all the teachings of the Western Roman Church; I was prohibited from speaking at all for a week and forced to fast every other day that same week. I realized reformation is impossible. The deception is embedded too deeply into these organizations that have blinded the eyes of their adherents."

"But we are a part of the Western Roman Church and have now rejected its false teachings and practices," Osbeorn said to John. "Many others will, too, if the truth is explained to them. Have you tried talking to the other monks in the monastery apart from Abbot Edwin?"

"I have not," John replied with his eyes downcast. "I guess I should. Please pray that the Lord gives me the courage to do so and puts the right words in my mouth. Also, my absence today was probably noticed. I will be subject to intense questioning and may be punished more severely. Please pray for me."

"Nothing is impossible with God," Priscilla responded. "Maybe He put you there to use you to change the Roman Church and therefore the whole world. Don't miss that great opportunity."

"I'm sorry Priscilla, but that won't happen," Barzillai said to Priscilla.

"How can you be so sure?" asked Simon.

"I think the Roman Church is Babylon the great, the mother of harlots and of abominations of the earth," replied Barzillai. "Exactly as written in the Book of Revelation."

"Interesting," exclaimed John, rubbing his chin, as the rest looked at Barzillai with bewildered expressions. "The infamously sinful Pope John XII[12] and Pope Benedict IX[13] come to mind."

"Let me read to you from the Book of Revelation," said Barzillai, before walking to the two large codices containing an Englisċ translation of Scripture.

After reading the passage corresponding to Revelation chapter 17, Barzillai explained, "The city that ruled over the kings of the earth when Revelation was written is none other than Rome. In the Old Testament, Israel's relationship with God was often symbolically referred to as a marriage covenant relationship, and Israel was called a harlot for worshipping false gods. The prophets, Hosea, Isaiah, Jeremiah, and Ezekiel talk about it a lot. But God is still faithful and is waiting for His people to return to Him. Israel will be given another chance, as Paul mentions in his Letter to the Romans."

"But doesn't it say that Babylon is the city which rules over the kings of the earth, meaning Rome itself?" questioned Thomas. "The Western Roman Empire, whose capital was Rome, collapsed hundreds of years ago, and the people who belong to the 'Roman Church' don't worship false gods. So the prophecy may have already been fulfilled when the pagan state religion was replaced by Christianity."

"By speaking about Rome, it refers to Rome's entire sphere of influence, which is now the Roman Church," said Barzillai. "And it was a mystery, as mentioned in the passage, because although there was a church in Rome, what we now call the Roman Church hadn't yet come into existence. The Apostle John, who wrote the Book of Revelation, would never have thought that there would come a time when a large part of the Church would become affiliated with the government that was persecuting them. It surely was a great relief for Christians who were being persecuted when Emperor Constantine patronized the Church and made it a state organization. The leaders who were not vigilant enough to guard against worldly power and wealth, however, easily became victims to the schemes of the evil one. False teachings were already rampant by the time Constantine became a Christian. Political power corrupted this organization even further. In the beginning of Lamentations, we will see that when Jerusalem is spoken about, it applies to the entire Kingdom of Judah. And remember, the passage I read to you from the Book of Revelation stated that Babylon was sitting on the beast, who is the Anti-Christ of the end times; this implies that the two would be hand in hand initially. But later on, the Anti-Christ and the ten kings who will give him their power and authority, will destroy Babylon. How could the pagan Roman Empire be called a harlot in the spiritual sense, like Israel and Judah were called harlots? As for the people in the Roman churches committing idolatry, they have idols of saints and angels, and they pray to saints and angels, which is equal to worshipping them. Whether it is praying, venerating, or worshipping, any such honor is to be given to God and God alone. Pagans are also idol worshippers, but the Roman Church has the honor and privilege of having the written word of God at their fingertips. Therefore, what they are doing cannot be excused as ignorance."

Barzillai then read aloud from the passage corresponding to Ezekiel 6:9 from the other codex, where God says: "Then those of you who escape will remember Me among the nations to which they will be carried captive, how I have been hurt by their adulterous hearts which turned away from Me, and by their eyes, which played the harlot after their idols; and they will loathe themselves in their own sight for the evils which they have committed, for all their abominations."

"I don't mean any disrespect, Barzillai, but isn't it possible that you are wrong about something here?" asked Simon. "I mean, the passage you read said that Babylon was drunk with the blood of the saints, but how many saints has the Roman Church killed?"

"Yes," Barzillai said, sighing. "I could be wrong about something. But did you know that the Roman Church has been persecuting believers who are not a part of it for hundreds of years? They group us together with true heretics and label us all 're-baptizing heretics.' And I think the persecution will only increase. Regardless of anyone being a heretic or not, Christians have no mandate to kill, but to love, even our enemies, as commanded by the Lord. God says, 'Come out of her, my people'. I hope everyone of you will leave Babylon this week."

After the discussion, Barzillai hid the codices of the Old Testament and the New Testament under the floor; there was a hidden hatch which led to a small room filled with old codices of various sizes containing portions of the Bible.

After this Barzillai took them to his house. It was about as big as Thomas' house. He invited them all inside. Deborah had prepared enough food for all of them.

"Once again, please don't hesitate to visit us and ask questions," Barzillai told them before they left his house.

"Wait, are you going to baptize us in a stream in the middle of winter?" Priscilla asked Barzillai. "Surely the water will be too cold, even if it is not frozen."

"Don't worry," Barzillai answered. "I will baptize you in a large tub in a house, and the water will be heated a little bit so it won't be too cold."

After saying goodbye to Barzillai and to those who wouldn't be walking in the same direction, they all returned home. Dermont and Cleena walked with Simon, Priscilla, and Zebedee. To his pleasant surprise, Zebedee could not detect any acrimony in Dermont's and Cleena's voices or on their faces as they spoke along the way.

"Zebedee, can we talk to you privately?" Cleena asked Zebedee after he said goodbye to her.

"Surely," he replied, his mind racing as he wondered what would come next.

"We forgive you," Dermont and Cleena said to Zebedee after Simon and Priscilla went inside their house.

Zebedee smiled and sighed with relief.

"When did God tell you that He wants you to stay celibate forever?" Cleena questioned Zebedee.

"It was a Friday," Zebedee answered, calculating the date. "The Friday after you and your father became Christians. November 17, I think."

"Oh," exclaimed Cleena and Dermont as they glanced at each other with surprised faces.

"So you didn't do anything wrong then," Cleena exclaimed.

After once again bidding Cleena and Dermont farewell, Zebedee went inside his parents' house.

"What are you waiting for, son?" Priscilla asked. "She obviously loves you. When are you going to propose?"

"You can sell your sword and shield to buy her jewelry," Simon suggested.

"God told me to stay celibate forever," said Zebedee calmly.

"What?" they asked.

At least they are not as surprised as they were when Jacobus and I told them that God brought Thomas back to life, Zebedee thought to himself. *That is a good sign. I thought they would be greatly dismayed.*

Priscilla put her face in her hands and began to bawl. Simon held her in his arms.

"Zebedee, what did you do?" Simon asked his youngest son, raising his voice.

"What do you mean?" asked Zebedee, trying to keep calm. "I am not lying."

"I know," yelled Simon. "What sin did you commit that God is punishing you this way?"

Zebedee was stupefied and appalled at the suggestion that he was being punished for some sin. He kept opening and closing his mouth, not knowing what to say at that moment.

"It is not because of sin," he finally said. "God told me that He has given me the gift of celibacy because of a special calling, and I trust He will help me to do His will."

"Is God punishing us, then?" Simon asked. "We lost your sister, and then John became a monk. Now you have to remain celibate too? You are adding to our sorrow."

Hearing this, Zebedee left the house to go for a walk to cool down.

Meanwhile, as John entered his room at the monastery, he was surprised to see Abbot Edwin inside. The abbot had a stern expression on his face and was standing beside John's codices, quill pens, and inkwells.

"Greetings, Abbot," John said, beginning to sweat and tremble a little bit.

The abbot did not respond. He simply stared at John.

John calmed down but did not know what to say.

"Why weren't you there during the worship service and afternoon meal?" queried the abbot, clearly suppressing his anger. "And why are you translating the Bible into Englisc?"

The abbot had apparently guessed that John had been planning on translating the Bible into Englisc because he wrote "New Testament" on the cover of one of the codices and wrote "Gospel of Matthew" on the top of the first page, in Englisc.

"So that people who can only read Englisć or aren't fluent in Latin can read it," John answered with sparkling eyes and a slight smile.

"Do you remember asking me why we don't translate the Bible into the vernacular a couple of years ago?" asked the abbot.

"Yes," John replied.

"And what did I say?" asked the abbot, whose face and voice were no longer hiding his ire.

"You said that the Church strongly discourages it because if the laity read the Bible for themselves they will misunderstand a lot of it, and that it would lead to them having false beliefs," John replied. "And that it would ultimately lead to divisions in the Church."

"Exactly," exclaimed Abbot Edwin. "So my answer was, 'No,', and I explained to you very clearly why it was 'No.'"

"But even if all of the teachings of either the Western or the Eastern Roman churches were accurate, those reasons would not be good enough," John responded calmly. "Jesus Christ our Lord Himself chose mostly illiterate men to be His disciples instead of scribes and teachers of the Law. Also, the seed must be sown, even though there are different soil types, as our Lord mentioned in the parable of the sower. And moreover, God the Holy Spirit will open the eyes of the people according to His will."

"Roman churches?" queried Abbot Edwin.

"There are no good reasons for not letting people read the Bible for themselves," John continued, ignoring the abbot's query.

"How are those not good reasons?" Abbott Edwin asked. "I have never met such a conceited man in my life. You think you understand the Scriptures better than everyone else? And what do you mean by Roman churches? Well, I know what you mean, but why are you calling them that? The Eastern Church is not Roman in any sense of the word. Its capital is Constantinople."

"What is the capital of the Eastern Roman Empire?" asked John.

"Fine," said the abbot. "The title 'Roman churches' is fine, but how is avoiding divisions not a good enough reason to keep the Bible away from the hands of the laity?"

"Even with keeping the Bible out of the hands of the laity, the Roman Church split into two almost equal parts," said John. "Ha! What do you have to say about that?"

"Exactly!" said the abbot. "Imagine all the divisions that would occur if the Bible was put into the hands of the laity."

"No one can fully understand the Bible," replied John. "But even if a lot of people break away from the Roman churches after reading the Bible for themselves and then further divide into dozens of smaller groups, the vast majority of those groups would understand the Bible better, and would follow it more closely, than the vast majority of the clergy of the Roman churches do."

"Hmm," said the abbot, rubbing his chin. "So you are not so conceited after all, but you are still wrong. Let me read to you from the Apostle Paul's First Letter to the Corinthians."

Abbot Edwin then picked up the codex which contained a Koine Greek copy of the New Testament that John had previously been planning to translate and read aloud the passage corresponding to 1 Corinthians 1:10, which says: "Now I exhort you, brethren, by the name of our Lord Jesus Christ, that you all agree, and there be no divisions among you, but you be made complete in the same mind and in the same judgment."

"The Apostle Paul did not mean that they should compromise and agree with false teachings for the sake of unity," shouted John. "You always have to read the Scriptures in context. Remember telling me this, Abbot? Paul goes on to say that he heard that some were saying that they are of Paul and some were saying that they are of Cephas, who is the Apostle Peter, and some were saying that they are of Apollos. Just some were saying that they are of Christ, which is what they all should have been saying, instead of fighting over which of His servants was the best preacher. Today, the Western Roman Church follows the bishop of Rome while the Eastern Roman Church follows the archbishop of Constantinople. As you read the Apostle Paul's letters, you will see that he wanted them all to read the Scripture that they had, which included his letters, to discern between false teachings and true teachings. There were some false teachings creeping in among the Corinthians, the Colossians, the Galatians, the Thessalonians, and others, and Paul was writing to them to dispel those false teachings."

Abbot Edwin was clearly amazed at the answer and could not respond.

"Please, Abbot Edwin," pleaded John. "Please try to understand the Bible, putting aside the teachings of the Roman Church. Just use the Bible to interpret the Bible and ask the Holy Spirit to help you understand the Bible. Seek the truth and you will find it. Don't be too proud to accept that a lot of what you believe is wrong."

"You said we are saved by God's grace alone and through our faith in Christ alone, and not by any works," Abbot Edwin said. "I told you to read Jacobus' [James'] epistle and you will see that it is just the beginning, and that we need to do good works to be fully saved and to go to Heaven. Your flawed understanding of what Jacobus was saying is that true faith produces good works, and our good works have no part in saving us. If you use the Bible to interpret the Bible without the teachings of the Church, you will end up with fallacious conclusions like these."

"Your conclusions are erroneous," John retorted. "Regardless of what you read in the Bible, you believe that the accepted teachings of the Western Roman Church are correct, because you think the pope is infallible and inerrant. That is the real fallacy. You twist Scripture to mean what you want it to mean, instead of letting the Bible interpret the Bible. The Bible is sufficient for all doctrines pertaining to faith and morals. By the way, you have still not been able to show me where the Bible says you can pray to saints in Heaven or angels or anyone apart from God."

"In the Book of Revelation we read about angels and saints in Heaven offering the prayers of the saints to God," replied the abbot.

"You have to remember that the Book of Revelation utilizes symbolism to depict actual facts," John responded. "The angel you are referring to only offers incense to God along with the prayers of the saints; it does not imply that he is offering the prayers of the saints. And remember to whom were those prayers directed? Our prayers to God are like sweet smelling incense to Him. Angels and saints in Heaven may say amen to our thanksgiving, praise, and worship given to God when we pray aloud and when they hear us, but that doesn't mean we can pray to them or through them. We mustn't forget that God loves the saints on Earth just as much as He loves the saints in Heaven. Just for the sake of argument: If a hundred people in a hundred different cities pray to the same saint or angel at the same time, how can that saint or angel listen to all those prayers? Angels and saints in Heaven are not omniscient, omnipresent, or all-hearing. God alone is."

After saying this, John heard some muttering not far behind him. He turned around to see a group of monks who resided in the abbey listening to the conversation right outside his room door.

"That's enough," said the old abbot. "Bartholomew and Nathaniel, I want you to escort John out of the monastery. He is not allowed in here ever again! I will let the Prior of Lewisham Priory know not to let him in either. Wait, what am I thinking? I'll just have you excommunicated."

"It makes no difference for me now," replied John.

John wanted to say what he was thinking, *I was going to inform you that I am leaving the monastery this very day. I am also leaving the Roman Church. The true Church of Christ is made up of every true believer in Heaven and on Earth, it is not a visible organization controlled by mere men,* but he knew doing so could lead not only to his execution, but also the execution of his family if they were interrogated.

"Of course there is," said the abbot. "Get him out of here."

"Wait!" exclaimed John, as Bartholomew and Nathaniel each grabbed one of his arms. "My possessions. Please let me take my possessions."

"All right!" exclaimed Abbot Edwin. "Let him take his possessions."

"Thank you," exclaimed John, as Bartholomew and Nathaniel let him go.

John picked up the codex in which he had begun writing, in his left hand, and another codex in his right hand.

"What?" asked the abbot.

"Can I come back for the rest?" asked John. "Or will someone help me carry them out?"

"These belong to yoouuu?" asked Abbot Edwin, astonished.

"Yes," replied John, with a large smile. "Someone bought them for me."

"I cannot let you take them, in case you somehow find a way to translate even parts of the Bible into Englisċ," explained Abbot Edwin.

"Abbot, are you going to steal my codices?" John asked him in a mocking tone. "How am I going to do that anyway?"

Maybe I shouldn't have used that tone, John immediately thought to himself.

"Oh, I am not going to steal it, I'm just going to burn it," replied the abbot.

"How can you burn them without first stealing them from me?" asked John.

"Joseph, bring me a torch!" the abbot commanded another monk who had entered the room.

"Wait!" John shouted desperately. "I will donate one codex to the abbey if you let me take these two safely."

"Hmm," said the abbot, rubbing his chin as he pondered the deal. "We really do need another large codex, but we can't afford to buy one yet. And you haven't really translated anything. Fine, John, we have a deal. You take whatever you can carry with you, since you can never enter Westminster Abbey again. The rest of your possessions will be left as donations to the abbey."

"Thank you, Edwin," John responded cheerfully, knowing this leniency was unusual in monasteries.

John carried the codices which were in his hands between his arms and his sides to free up his hands; then he picked up a full inkwell with his left hand and his unused quill pens with his right hand. All the monks nearby walked beside John as he headed toward the front door of the abbey. John was the only one smiling. John took a deep breath as he stepped out of the monastery for the final time. He smiled as he heard the doors close behind him. He had left Babylon!

"Zebedee," John called out to his youngest brother, who happened to be close to the cathedral.

Zebedee, who was still a little upset, recognized his oldest brother's voice, looked in the direction the voice came from, and spotted a cheerful John who had his hands full. The sight made Zebedee chuckle and forget about what upset him. Zebedee ran to John, who was walking towards him.

"Brother, am I glad to see you!" exclaimed John. "I need help carrying these things to our parents' house."

"Sure," Zebedee said, taking the codex and inkwell from John's left hand.

CHAPTER 10

SCRIPTURAL PROOF

Zebedee and John informed the rest of the group of twenty-eight, as well as Barzillai and his household, what happened that very day.

From that day onward, John began going to Barzillai's house every day. The two of them then went to the chapel to make another copy of an Engliśc translation of the Bible from the copies there.

John left his codices in the chapel so he did not need to carry them there every day, which certainly would have made him conspicuous, as he walked down the streets of London.

"Greetings, brothers and sisters," announced Barzillai as the church service began the following Sunday, January 7, 1067. "I am going to baptize the newest members of our congregation who are eight years or older today after the service. You are all welcome to come with us and I hope you all do."

After the service, Barzillai and Deborah led the congregation out of the city, much to Zebedee's surprise.

The young men took turns carrying barrels. There were two barrels filled with bread and the third had a bow, two quivers full of arrows, and two torches.

"Why are we going out of the city?" Zebedee asked Barzillai.

"So that no one who knows us, sees us," answered Barzillai. "If we are reported to the authorities, we will all be put to death, man, woman, and child."

Barzillai baptized the new members in Peter's house, which was not very far from the city. Inside, there was a large tub filled with water which was made just for baptisms. The others cheered, clapped, praised God, and congratulated those who had just been baptized.

After the baptisms, they ate the bread from the barrels and fruits from nearby trees. Two of the men went hunting and brought in some game, while a few others were preparing fires for cooking the meat. Then Zebedee and his brothers started gutting, skinning, cleaning, and butchering the deer, and those who lit the fires cooked the meat.

"Now I am going to show the new members of our congregation our underground repository," Barzillai announced after everyone had eaten their fill. "The rest of you are free to go to your houses or to come with us, as you please."

Barzillai then took the two torches from the barrel and gave one of them to John.

"Light the torch in the fire and walk in the middle of the group," Barzillai instructed John before lighting the torch he was holding.

Those who were interested in going to the repository formed a line with Barzillai at the front and John in the middle.

"What kind of repository is it?" Zebedee asked Barzillai along the way.

"Let's see if you can guess," exclaimed Barzillai with a smile.

"A library?" Clement asked.

"You are right," exclaimed Barzillai, excitedly.

"What kind of...?" Zebedee stopped before saying the word "books" because it was obvious.

They stopped in the middle of a meadow. Barzillai bent down, felt for something on the ground, and opened a door hidden by the grass.

"This is very important," Barzillai announced as he stepped onto the first step leading down the hole. "The last person has to close the door behind them. I will light every other torch in the tunnel and John will light the ones I don't."

The short staircase led to a tunnel where there were some unlit torches along the walls; the tunnel led to an underground cavern, which also had some unlit torches.

"My ancestors used to gather here before the chapel we now use was abandoned," Barzillai stated. "We have several copies of the books of the Bible here. The congregation still comes here to borrow and return codices and scrolls."

Barzillai then took them to a corner of the cavern that had a large shelf containing many small and medium sized codices and scrolls that looked very old.

"Every household may borrow one scroll or codex at a time," Barzillai declared. "Please handle them carefully and return them as soon as you can after reading them. And remember, just because you have already read a book in the Bible doesn't mean you shouldn't read it again. Many of the adults in our congregation have read the entire Bible multiple times."

"Why aren't we evangelizing more?" John asked Barzillai that Friday. "I know that we will be persecuted if caught, but we don't have to preach publicly on the streets. All of us have many friends, and some of us have many relatives who have not heard the true gospel of Jesus Christ. Shouldn't we at least tell them what the Bible really says, privately?"

"You have no idea how much my ancestors were persecuted by the Roman Church," Barzillai replied, obviously suppressing his frustration. "Ultimately, all our preaching, wise words and arguments, and even exposition of the Bible, aren't enough to convince anyone. Jesus said that no one can come to Him unless the Father draws them, unless the Holy Spirit works in a person's heart, they cannot repent and believe the gospel. So we decided that we will just focus on obeying God and holy living. We don't even know whom to preach to. God alone knows who His elect are and He will save them."

"But we are commanded to go into all the world and preach the gospel to all nations," said John. "Christ died for the sins of the whole world. Paul and Peter let us know that God wants all to be saved. Was the persecution which your ancestors suffered at the hands of the Roman Church any worse than the persecution the Christians in the first three centuries of the Church age suffered at the hands of the Roman Empire? They preached the gospel knowing that they would face extreme persecution. Just look at how much the Apostle Paul suffered."

"By the way, my father preached to many of his friends," Barzillai retorted. "They all just mocked him. He lost many friends because of his preaching, and he did not win a single convert. Some seemed to believe for a while, but they never truly did. Thankfully, no one reported him to the authorities."

"I'm sure you have read this passage in Romans many times," said John, as he opened the New Testament codex to Paul's Letter to the Romans and began to read Romans 10:13-17 aloud. The passage reminds the reader that people cannot believe in Christ unless someone preaches the Gospel to them.

"If it was just my life at risk, I would evangelize," said Barzillai. "I would even be willing to preach aloud on the streets, but that would put my dear wife's life, and possibly the lives of everyone in this congregation, at risk."

"Jesus said that unless we love Him more than our father, mother, sister, brother, wife, son, daughter, and our own life, we are not worthy to be His disciples," John responded. "I know it is hard, but we need to depend on Him solely and totally, even for the strength to obey Him. We need to live for Him alone, not for anyone else."

"You are right, John," replied Barzillai, sighing. "Thank you for reminding this old man what he is supposed to do. Oh, I have been such a hypocrite."

That evening Barzillai spoke with Deborah about his conversation with John. Deborah agreed with them. Barzillai and Deborah prayed together and asked the Lord to forgive them for not doing all that He called them to do.

The following Sunday, Barzillai told the congregation about his conversation with John, and asked them to forgive him for not shepherding them well. Then he encouraged them all to actively share their faith and preach the Gospel.

"Invite your friends and relatives who love you to come here on Saturday morning at the same time that our Sunday meetings commence," Barzillai announced. "John and I will do our best to answer all their questions and enlighten them about the true teachings of the Bible. Pray that God opens their eyes, and please don't forget to ask the Lord to put the right words in your mouths and in ours."

That week almost everyone in the congregation reached out to at least one person with the gospel. Some evangelized to many. They spread the Word to their friends, relatives, employees, and coworkers.

The chapel was fuller that Saturday than it had ever been. All the believers who usually met there on Sundays, apart from John and Barzillai, had to stand outside.

I suppose this great turn out is because of Thomas being brought back to life and my knee being healed in York, as well as me selling my land and animals to give the money to the poor and then giving my house to Dermont and Cleena in obedience to the Lord, Zebedee thought to himself, as he stood in the cold outside. *I have to stand outside in this cold weather for who knows how long. I sure hope this meeting ends soon... Wait, what's wrong with me? How could I be so selfish? I am not the only one standing out here in the cold. I am a young man, and more importantly, I should exult. I should be jubilant that so many showed up to listen to the truth.*

O Lord God Almighty, please forgive me for my grumbling and selfishness, Zebedee prayed silently. *And thank you that so many people are here. Please fill me with Your compassion for them. Please open their eyes. Please fill John and Barzillai with the wisdom and courage they need.*

Zebedee noticed that many of those outside began to shiver and a few moments later he began to shiver as well.

When I place My children in challenging situations, I want them to call on Me for strength, the Lord spoke to Zebedee's heart.

Lord Jesus, please help us; we are shivering, Zebedee prayed. *We can't bear this freezing weather for much longer.*

Immediately, everyone stopped shivering. When Zebedee noticed this, he knew that the warmth that had just come over him must have come over them as well!

Thank you, Lord, Zebedee prayed in his mind, as his eyes briefly teared up with joy.

Meanwhile, inside the chapel, John began by saying, "My fellow citizens of Engla Land, greetings. As some of you know, I was a monk at Westminster Abbey not long ago. Upon carefully and thoroughly studying the Bible, I realized that neither the Western Roman Church nor the Eastern Roman

Church was following the Bible. It is for that reason alone that I had decided to leave the monastery the very day I was told to leave. I will still remain celibate forever to serve the Lord without distractions. Barzillai here is a descendant of the Jewish diaspora who were Christians. Barzillai has a copy of the entire Bible in Englisċ. I know none of you has heard the Bible read in Englisċ before. Have you ever wondered why? Barzillai will explain it to you, but first, we invite two of you who don't believe us and are able to read, to come here and confirm what we are saying."

"My husband and I will come," a woman announced from the crowd inside the chapel.

A few moments later, a woman and a man came to stand beside John and Barzillai. They were Alta's parents.

"Let me start by saying that salvation is by God's grace alone and through faith alone in Jesus Christ alone," Barzillai began, before reading the passages corresponding to John 3:16 and then 1 John 5:13 out loud. The passages make it clear that those who believe in Jesus Christ already have everlasting life.

"You see, everlasting life isn't something you can earn after death by doing good works, because no amount of good works is adequate to meet the righteous standards of God. A human receives everlasting life the moment they put their trust in the Lord Jesus Christ for salvation."

He then turned to Paul's Letter to the Ephesians and read Ephesians 2:8-9 out loud, which states we are saved by God's grace, through faith, and not by works, before reading from the passage corresponding to Galatians 5:4 aloud, which makes it clear that keeping the Law is not the way to attain salvation.

"It is not possible for someone who has been born again into the family of God and in whom the Holy Spirit dwells to be severed from Christ or to fall from grace," Barzillai elucidated. "I think Paul is just saying that if we have to keep the Law, in addition to having faith in Jesus to be saved, then we cannot be saved because we have broken the Law and will keep breaking it. Our good works don't nullify our sins. It is only by the blood of Jesus Christ that we can be forgiven of our sins. He took the full punishment for all our sins. God wants us to obey Him out of love for Him, not out of fear of going to hell."

"Barzillai and John must be taking passages out of context," said Alta's father, Tata, who was reading along. "That is assuming that they are reading an accurate translation of the Bible."

"How could you say that?" asked Angus. "He read from multiple passages, and it is so clear, but why don't you read the context for yourself and enlighten the rest of us?"

Alta's parents went through what was written before and after the passages that were quoted but couldn't find any discrepancies.

"I think you can continue," Angus told Barzillai and John.

There was some murmuring inside the chapel.

"In his Letter to the Galatians, Paul makes it clear that being circumcised is not necessary to be saved, or better in any way, than not being circumcised," John declared. "The clergy of the Roman churches may say that 'Paul was only referring to the ceremonial laws in the Old Testament, which only applied to the Jews and not to us, but keeping the rest is necessary for obtaining salvation.'

"However, that doesn't make any sense. The Law is the Law. If you keep reading Paul's Letter to the Galatians, you will see that Paul makes it clear that we cannot be saved by the Law; the Law only shows us our guilt, and our need for Christ and His forgiveness. We are saved by God's grace, through our faith in Jesus Christ. Paul admonishes the Galatians not to take advantage of the freedom that they have in Christ by giving in to their sinful desires. He tells them that if they are truly in Christ, they will love one another instead of following their sinful desires."

"Even if they are correct about this, it would not prove that we should leave the so called Western Roman Church," exclaimed Alta's mother, Tabitha. "The clergy are imperfect men, and they are still figuring things out."

"The clergy clearly either lack understanding or the ability to tell the truth," replied Angus. "Isn't that proof enough that we can't just blindly follow them?"

"Is there anything else you would like to tell us?" asked Tata. "You must be hiding something. Go ahead, tell us about all your teachings that differ from the teachings of the Church."

"We are not taking any Scripture passages out of context," announced Barzillai. "And you need to know that the true Church of Christ is composed of all true believers in Heaven and on Earth. It is not a visible organization like the Roman churches, which were made and are governed by mere men. Christ Himself is the Head of the true Church and is the Rock on which it is built. He has no vicar on earth. By the way, all true believers are saints and priests, and Christ Himself is our Great High Priest. Have you been told that we shouldn't pray to anyone apart from God? Not even saints or angels? We can confidently approach the throne of God by the blood and in the name of Jesus Christ, for He is the only mediator between God and man, being both fully God and perfect Man."

Upon hearing this, those gathered inside began to murmur once again. They were clearly astonished.

"I can't believe it," shouted Tata. "This man is not only blaspheming against the pope, the saints, and God's holy angels, but against God Himself! How can we, being sinners, directly approach the throne of God?"

"Nothing Barzillai just said is false," John replied. "Let me read to you from the epistle to the Hebrews and the epistle to the Colossians. Please give me a minute to find the passages."

John read the passages corresponding to Hebrews 4:14-16, which states that Jesus Christ is our Great High Priest and we can approach God's throne with confidence through Him, and Colossians 2:18, which states false humility and worship of angels is wrong.

"You may think you are being humble by believing you need to pray to or through saints and angels sometimes, but that is false humility," Barzillai said. "Our God and Savior Jesus Christ has shed His own blood so that we can have a personal intimate relationship with God."

"I am tired of hearing Scripture taken out of context," Tata yelled. "That must be what you are doing. Once again, I am assuming that your Englisċ translation of the Bible is an accurate translation; I am not sure whether it is or isn't, but I am giving you the benefit of the doubt."

"It is appalling how the Church, I mean the organized churches, directly contradict Scripture," Angus retorted in astonishment. "How and why did the Roman Church go so much astray from the Bible?"

"Either because they didn't bother reading the Bible or they didn't care about what it said," answered Barzillai. "Also, they were influenced by pagan religions around them. And as I tell you more of their wrong teachings, you will discover other reasons like greed and selfish ambition, as well as using their own logic instead of taking Scripture for what it says. They also added to the Book of Daniel and the Book of Esther in the Old Testament and added a few books into the Old Testament; one of those books, the Book of Tobit, has someone praying for the dead and giving alms for the dead, but those teachings cannot be found anywhere in the Bible. You see, our prayers won't help the souls of the people being tormented in Hades, and the souls of the people in Heaven don't need our prayers. And giving alms to the poor will not purge away the sins of anyone, either dead or alive. Even in the Old Testament, good works did not take away anyone's sins. The blood of Jesus Christ is the only thing that can wash away one's sins."

"How do you know that those books don't belong in the Bible?" Tabitha asked, scoffing. "To me it sounds like you just removed the things you don't like."

"Well, apart from what Barzillai already said, not everyone in the Roman churches is completely sure whether those books belong to the inspired Scriptures or not," stated John. "And secondly...give me a moment...I cannot remember exactly where the passage is..."

Once again he was trying to find another passage in Scripture. This time it took him longer than usual. Once he found it he read Romans 3:1-2 aloud, which states that the oracles of God were given to the Jews.

"Since the Jews don't have those extra books in their Scriptures, we know that those books aren't part of the Old Testament." John continued. "And they are definitely not part of the New Testament because they talk about events that happened before the New Testament times. If you still aren't totally sure that they aren't inspired by God, listen to this. Those books not only have doctrinal errors, but also have historical errors. In the Book of Judith, it says Nebuchadnezzar was the king of the Assyrians and ruled from Nineveh. But the truth is, Nebuchadnezzar was the king of Babylon. As the emperor of the Babylonian Empire, he ruled over the Assyrians as well, so he was the king of the Assyrians as well. But he did not rule from the city of Nineveh. Babylon was under the Assyrian Empire till Nebuchadnezzar's father, Nabopolassar, rebelled against the Assyrian Empire and burned its capital,__Nineveh, to the ground. There was no Nineveh when Nebuchadnezzar inherited his father's throne."

Gasps of bewilderment rose from many gathered in the chapel.

"There are a lot more errors in those books and passages," John continued. "The authors probably just wanted to make interesting historical fiction stories with the intention of teaching a moral lesson."

Now everyone chuckled, but then realized that John was serious. He really believed what he said. It wasn't a joke.

"In the Book of Baruch, the people of Judah are told that they would be captives in Babylon for seven generations," John remarked. "But in the Book of Jeremiah, the people of Judah are told that God said they would be captives in Babylon for seventy years. History tells us that God fulfilled what He spoke through His servant Jeremiah.

"And in the Book of Wisdom, a man says his soul received an undefiled body because it was good. But the truth is, all our bodies were defiled from the moment we were conceived in our mother's womb, which is when our souls came into existence."

"Nowhere in the Bible, or in the books and passages added by the Roman Church, is there any mention of an intermediate place where believers go after death, to be purified by fire before they can go to Heaven," Barzillai added. "But since our prayers obviously won't affect those in Heaven or those in Hades, the Western Roman Church concluded that there is another place where believers go when they die, to be purified of their sins. But the Bible tells us that Jesus Christ our Lord suffered the full punishment for all our sins on the cross, and there is nothing else other than the blood of Jesus that can cleanse us from our sins."

"What is the purpose of baptism, the Eucharist, and alms if salvation is received by faith alone?" Tabitha protested.

"Baptism doesn't save you or make you a member of the Church or remove your sinful nature, which the Western Roman Church calls 'original sin'," Barzillai began. "By the way, although it may be fine to use the term 'original sin', it is called 'flesh' in the Bible. Our congregation calls it our 'sinful nature' or 'tendency to sin' when talking about it, so that no one gets confused between our sinful nature and our physical flesh. Now, back to baptism. True water baptism, which is an external affirmation of the baptism by the Holy Spirit, should be done by full immersion. The ancient Koine Greek word for baptism means immersion. Baptism is supposed to be an outward sign that shows what already happened in your heart. You need to be saved first, to be baptized, not the other way around. Baptism is for believers, not for babies. As for communion, the bread and the wine just symbolize Christ's body and blood, respectively; communion does not save us, is not a sacrifice, and should only be taken by those who are saved. It does not impart…"

"Wait, hold on a minute," interrupted Tabitha. "Can you please prove what you are saying is Scriptural?"

"Surely," replied Barzillai. "I was planning to do that in a minute anyway."

Once again he began searching for a passage in the Bible. The rest waited patiently.

Barzillai read the passage corresponding to Acts chapter 10 out loud.

"As you just heard in this passage, Cornelius and his relatives and close friends received the Holy Spirit, implying they put their faith in Jesus and were saved, while the Apostle Peter was telling them the gospel, and only after that were they baptized," said Barzillai. "Baptism symbolizes that we died with Christ and rose again to new life with Him spiritually, and that one day our bodies will be resurrected just like His was. By the way, the thief on the cross expressed his faith in Jesus and was saved. This makes it clear that we receive salvation through faith in Christ, and not by any other means."

"I think we should also read the beginning of 1 Corinthians to them," John said to Barzillai.

"You are right, John," Barzillai agreed and read the Scripture from the passage corresponding to 1 Corinthians 1:1-17 aloud.

"Paul states he is writing to saints," John pointed out. "Yet he only baptized a few of them and said that he was sent to preach the gospel, not to baptize. How much clearer can it be that we receive God's gift of salvation through faith in Christ and not through being baptized with water?"

"How did the Roman churches get it backwards?" Angus asked. It didn't seem like he was expecting an answer. "It is as clear as day."

Barzillai replied, "It is understandable why they got confused about this and thought that water baptism is necessary for salvation. They failed to read the Scriptures in context. It is the baptism of the Holy Spirit that saves you. One is baptized with the Holy Spirit when they call on the name of Christ, with true repentance and faith, for salvation. When reading the Bible, it is important to look at the context of the passage and the book in which it is found; we also need to take into consideration whether the book is in the Old Testament or the New Testament. Since we are saved by grace alone and through faith alone, it is clear we don't need any rituals or good works to be saved, but the Bible also makes it clear repeatedly that if we truly have faith in the Lord Jesus Christ, our life will show it. Near the end of his First Letter to the Corinthians, Paul mentions that some are baptized for the dead. Paul neither encourages nor discourages the practice. Let me read it for you."

After finding the passage Barzillai read aloud 1 Corinthians 15:29, which states some people are baptized for the dead.

"How does that make any sense?" Tabitha questioned. "How can someone be saved after death?"

"Exactly," Barzillai answered. "This proves that water baptism does not save, it is just a sign and a public profession of faith."

"But why did they start baptizing infants?" Angus inquired.

"Because they thought that water baptism is necessary for salvation and they didn't know that when a baby dies he or she goes straight to Heaven," Barzillai answered. "Even if a baby did hear the gospel, how much would he or she understand? God is a just Judge and God is Love."

The sound that came from those gathered inside was hard to describe, they were overwhelmed by the tender love of God. A lot of them became teary eyed.

"How about communion?" Angus asked. "What made them think it was necessary for salvation?"

"There is a passage in the Gospel of John where Jesus says that He is the bread from heaven and that those who eat His flesh and drink His blood will have everlasting life, and that His flesh is true food and His blood is true drink," Barzillai responded. "But Jesus wasn't talking about communion. He said this much before His last supper, which was the first communion. He wasn't saying that the bread and wine literally become His body and blood, and He wasn't saying that communion was necessary for salvation. Just like we need to eat to survive in this life, we need to depend on Jesus for everlasting life. If you read the passage in context it is clear that eating His flesh and drinking His blood means believing in Him and depending on Him for abundant and everlasting life, which starts from the moment of conversion. The Old Testament forbids eating human flesh and drinking any blood."

"I think it is also necessary to mention that while the New Testament clearly states it is better to be celibate than it is to get married, it does not forbid marriage for those in leadership roles in the Church," John added. "In fact, the Apostle Paul calls humans forbidding marriage for other humans a doctrine of demons. God alone has the right to forbid marriage for someone."

Gasps of bewilderment rose from those gathered in the chapel once more.

John then read aloud from the passage corresponding to 1 Timothy 3:1-4, which states that church overseers must not have more than one wife and should be above reproach, and 1 Timothy 4:1-5, which makes it clear that humans forbidding other humans form getting married and from eating certain foods are doctrines of demons.

"As most of you know," continued John, "the pope gave William his blessing to invade Engla Land because some priests in Engla Land are married and the pope wants to mandate celibacy for the clergy. By the way, if you think all monks and unmarried priests in Engla Land are chaste, you are wrong.[11]"

"Now that I know for sure that I am saved, I love God more," Zebedee interjected from outside the chapel. "I want to do what He wants me to do more than ever. When I didn't know about the assurance of salvation, I still tried to do what was right, but now I am living for God and God alone, with His empowerment."

There was a lot of murmuring inside the chapel once again.

"Is there anything else we need to know?" Angus asked.

"Yes," Barzillai answered. "Although Mary was very blessed by being Jesus' earthly mother, she is not more special than other Christians. She is not, and never was, the Mother of God. She is no longer Jesus' mother; and she and Joseph had at least six children together."

Barzillai then read the passage corresponding to Mark 6:3, which states the names of Jesus' mother, Mary, and brothers Jacobus, Joses, Judas, and Simon, and states Jesus had sisters.

"And she is not a queen," John added, "and her body decayed like the bodies of other first century Christians."

"That's enough," Tabitha shouted. "I have heard enough of this nonsense."

"Actually, it all makes sense," Angus retorted.

"Alright," said Barzillai. "I think we covered the main errors of the Roman Church. You will discover more as you keep coming here and read the Scriptures for yourselves. You can always ask me if you have any more questions."

"John, Barzillai, isn't there anything that you two disagree on?" Tata asked the two men who were holding a codex each. "I mean, there are lots of disagreements in the Western Roman Church itself. There always have been."

"Well, Barzillai believes it is wrong to kill another human, no matter what," John stated. "I don't believe it is wrong to kill another human to defend yourself and others."

"So what did you do when you were forced to join the fyrd?" Angus asked.

"I joined the fyrd, but I never killed anyone," Barzillai responded, and laughed. "If an enemy engaged me in combat, I just defended myself without hurting them, and by God's grace, I am still alive."

"Thank you very much, Barzillai, John, for explaining all this to us," Angus said.

"You are welcome," John and Barzillai replied. "Wait, we will have two services here tomorrow," Barzillai announced as people were beginning to leave. "The first one will begin at the beginning of the second tid of the day, just like the services at St. Paul's Cathedral, Eastminster, and St. Peter's Cathedral, Westminster; and the second one will begin at the beginning of the fourth tid of the day."

There were four "tids" in a day and four in the night, measured by a "tide dial" or a "scratch dial", and have nothing to do with the tides of water bodies.

CHAPTER 11

LAUGHTER AND SORROW

Two days later, at dusk, there was a knock on the front door of Simon's and Priscilla's house.

"They took my land," exclaimed Osbeorn, enraged, as Zebedee opened the door.

"What?" asked Zebedee. "Who took it? How?"

"Come in, friend," Simon said to Osbeorn. "Tell us what happened."

"King Will…no, William the Tyrant, stole the lands of all those who fought against him at Caldbec Hill," Osbeorn fumed. "We were just defending our king and country. He took the land I bought from Zebedee, as well, but returned it to me when I informed him that I did not own it back then, I took a loan to buy it, and that he should repay the loan if he doesn't give it back."

Osbeorn, Simon, Priscilla, and Zebedee couldn't help laughing at the last part.

"So you spoke to King William directly?" Zebedee asked, astounded.

"Yes," Osbeorn replied. "I was so angry that I demanded to speak to him myself, unsure if he would have my head for it."

They all laughed again.

"God is good," said Osbeorn, who had calmed down now. "My head is still attached to my neck and since I still have the land I bought from you, I am still a thegn."

"How much land does that greedy man want?" Priscilla asked.

"He is giving a lot of the stolen land to his nobles," Osbeorn exclaimed. "As you know, many of them have moved to Engla Land. You are fortunate you did not join Harold's army as you were sick."

The next morning, as Zebedee left his parents' house and was walking toward their farm, Eva approached him and asked, "What is wrong with you, Zebedee?"

"Huh?" Zebedee said. "What is it now, Eva?"

"Why did you reject such a beautiful woman?" she shrieked. "Are you blind?"

"What?" asked Zebedee. "I thought you would have moved on by now, and you are so full of yourself."

"I wasn't talking about myself," she said, "I was talking about Cleena. I have never seen someone more beautiful. Have you?"

"No, I haven't," Zebedee retorted. "So what? Leave me alone."

"God told you to, didn't He?" Eva questioned.

Zebedee's jaw dropped open.

"How do you know?" Zebedee queried.

"I thought so," she replied softly and look away. "There is no other explanation. So how do you do it?"

"Do what?" he asked.

"Devote your life to God like that?" she asked. "I know you love Cleena. People noticed you taking her on a tour around London. People know you sold your farm because God told you to, and then you gave her father your house after a storm destroyed his, and you moved back in to your parents' house. People also saw her cry on Christmas Day before the coronation. You are a war hero. Did you really think people wouldn't notice and wouldn't talk about these things? And now God won't even let you be with the one you love. How is that fair?"

"God is the one I love the most, because He loves me more than I could ever imagine," Zebedee responded. "Jesus took on human flesh for me. He suffered and died for me, so now I am living for Him. Even though I don't deserve to be happy, He gives me joy, true lasting joy. He has removed my romantic feelings for Cleena and I am glad you finally admit that God exists."

"Of course He exists," Eva said. "I didn't want to believe in Him because nuns and monks exist. They devote their lives to God and deprive themselves of the pleasures of this world. I could never deny myself and follow Jesus like that. I chose not to believe in God because I did not want to obey Him, but I don't want to go to hell."

"Salvation is a gift," Zebedee replied. "God wants us to love Him and obey Him out of our love for Him, not out of fear of going to hell."

"Yes, I have heard it, Alta told me," Eva said. "I could never believe that the elements of the Eucharist actually became the body and blood of Christ, or that unbaptized babies go to hell. I tried to convince myself that these nonsensical teachings prove that the Bible cannot be trusted, but Alta recently let me know that the Bible does not teach these things."

"Yes, everything Alta told you is true," Zebedee said.

"So how do I become a true Christian?" Eva asked.

"Just come to Jesus and surrender yourself to Him," Zebedee said. "Fall at His feet, fall into His arms. He enables me to live for Him. His Spirit dwells in me and empowers me to do all that He calls me to do. Ask Him to dwell in you and help you, too."

"Alright," Eva responded, softly. "Thank you, Zebedee. By the way, I fancied you from the moment I met you. Most women may think you are slightly ugly, but I think that you are so ugly that you are actually a little handsome."

Hearing this, Zebedee began to laugh.

"I was too shy and proud to admit it," Eva went on, "and I stopped fancying you right now because God told you to stay celibate forever."

I didn't know you could be shy and proud at the same time, Zebedee thought to himself, amused.

"I hope you don't mind my asking," Eva continued, "but are you glad that you can't get married and can't have children? Or do you wish you could?"

"Hmm," began Zebedee. "Now that you mention children, I guess I am even more glad God told me not to get married. I have heard a lot about how hard it is to raise up children, although I was always told it was worth it, but I don't feel that way. However, I know that God would have enabled me to do it if it were His will."

"How can you not want children?" Eva asked, shocked.

Zebedee chuckled.

"You're quite odd," she said and chuckled as well.

The following day, King William issued a decree stating that it was illegal for Anglo-Saxons to hunt, fish, or gather anything from forests or any area of land that he designated to be a forest. Only William and his Norman nobles were free to hunt, fish, and forage in forests or other hunting reserves. Even the Norman nobles couldn't hunt in forests or reserves which they did not own unless they were invited. This made life even more difficult for the Anglo-Saxons, especially for the poorest ceorls. Although the few ceorls who did hunt did so extremely rarely, most ceorls used to gather things like fruits, wood, and soil from the forests.

The next Sunday, Jacobus and Alta brought Eva and her parents to the chapel with them.

In the discussion during the service, Eva asked Barzillai, "Why hasn't Jesus come back yet?"

"God is waiting for more people to come to the knowledge of the truth, repent, and be saved," Barzillai answered. "And there are many prophecies in the Bible that need to be fulfilled before the Lord's return."

"Like what?" Eva inquired.

"Well," began Barzillai, "There are many prophecies about both the First Coming and the Second Coming of Christ from Genesis to Revelation. There are more prophecies about the Second Coming than about the First. I have studied the entire Bible several times to understand the signs of His Second Coming. Although Jesus said that the exact time is in God's hands, and no one knows it, He revealed to us many of the signs and events that would precede His Second Coming. According to my knowledge, God will bring a remnant of the Jews scattered throughout the world back to the land of Israel, and Israel will become a nation again. The Gospel will be preached to all nations. The Jews will build another temple in Jerusalem. There will be two witnesses prophesying in Israel for one thousand two hundred sixty days, which is about three and a half years. After that, the Anti-Christ will kill them in Jerusalem and desecrate the temple. God will bring the two prophets back to life three and a half days after their death and will call them up to Heaven. After entering the temple, the Anti-Christ will speak blasphemies against the God of Heaven and claim that he himself is the greatest god. Then begins the great tribulation. God's wrath will be poured out on the earth and those on earth will suffer more than any generation before them and any after. The great tribulation will last for about three and a half years."

"Then what?" Zebedee asked. "The second coming?"

Peter replied by quoting Matthew 24:29-30, which states that there will be great signs in the sun, moon, and stars immediately after the tribulation.

Those who didn't know Peter well were amazed that he had memorized that passage, and those who had neither read nor heard it before were astonished by it.

"That's frightening," Cleena said. "I hope I die before the great tribulation begins."

"Christians are not appointed to wrath," Barzillai announced, and quoted the passage corresponding to 1 Thessalonians 5:9. "We will not face the wrath of God. However, Christians will be intensely persecuted during the great tribulation. But don't worry, at least some believers in the early church believed that the millennium reign of Christ will be a Sabbath after six thousand years since the creation of the world, or the creation of man. And those things happened roughly five thousand years ago. This is my notion, but the timings are in God's hands."

"So are you saying you think the Lord will come again roughly one thousand years from now?" Priscilla asked.

"Yes," Barzillai replied.

"But we could be wrong," Deborah added.

"Yes, we could be," Barzillai agreed.

"We must eagerly look forward to Jesus' Second Coming," Deborah continued. "And we never know which day will be our last, so we should always be ready to stand before Him so that we are not ashamed when we finally behold His face."

One Saturday afternoon, the next month, Jacobus and Alta came to Simon and Priscilla's house weeping. Zebedee was there, as well.

"Alta's parents said that they just discovered that Alta is my second cousin once removed," Jacobus began, while sobbing. "They said that they will report it to the church tribunal to annul the marriage next week and are giving us time to accept it and prepare to separate."

Jacobus and Alta then began crying again and hugged each other.

"How can this be?" Simon asked, astonished.

"They must be lying," exclaimed Priscilla, who was also astonished. "I think we would know if that were the case."

"You are right," Simon replied, "but we will need to prove it. But what if, somehow, Alta actually is Jacobus' second cousin once removed? What do we do then? What does the Bible say?"

"That's right," exclaimed Priscilla. "The Western Roman Church probably isn't following the Bible in this matter either. John and Barzillai will know what to do. Let's go to the chapel immediately."

The five of them went to the chapel and informed Barzillai and John about the situation.

"Hmm," said John. "I think they are lying."

"I do too," said Barzillai. "I have heard of an incident like this before and it was a fabrication intended to end a marriage because both spouses wanted a divorce. But this time it is the parents of one of the spouses doing this to end a happy marriage against their child's wishes. Regardless of whether Jacobus and Alta are really so closely related or not, there is absolutely no need to worry."

"What?" exclaimed Jacobus, Alta, Simon, Priscilla, and Zebedee simultaneously.

John and Barzillai laughed. The other five in the chapel were relieved but exchanged confused glances with each other.

"The Bible does not prohibit even first cousin marriage, although I think it is implied that the Israelites discouraged it, at least while they were following the Law," Barzillai said. "Marriage was instituted by God. It is not an invention by man. Man cannot change the definition of marriage."

Barzillai then quoted Matthew 19:4-6, which states that what God has joined together, let no man separate.

"And what is the pope going to do, even if you are within seven degrees of kinship?" John asked Jacobus and Alta. "Excommunicate you? Oh, wait, you already left his apostate church."

"You will not be breaking the law of Engla Land by not divorcing Alta, even if the Western Roman Church commands you to," Barzillai said. "So you have absolutely no need to worry."

Alta and Jacobus sighed with relief.

"Should we go to your parents' house or invite them here?" Barzillai asked Alta.

"Umm," said Alta. "I don't know…"

"I think we should invite them here," said John. "That way we can read to them from the Bible without having to carry a large codex to their house and then back here."

"You're right," Barzillai responded.

"Come on Alta, let's go," Jacobus said to his wife as he clasped her hand.

Jacobus and Alta brought Tata and Tabitha to the chapel.

"Can you please show us the document which you claim proves that Alta is Jacobus' second cousin once removed?" Barzillai asked Tata and Tabitha.

"Here it is," said Tata as he handed a piece of parchment to Barzillai. "It is a letter from my great-grandmother to Simon's grandfather. She informs him that she bore him a child. He was married at the time and she was a widow."

Barzillai read the document and then handed it to John, laughing.

"Well, John, what do you think?" Barzillai asked.

"Wait," said John as he began reading it. "This ink looks like it is not more than a few days old."

"Exactly," said Barzillai, who was well-versed with how parchments look. "And the parchment itself doesn't look like it is more than a couple years old."

Everyone apart from Tata, Tabitha, and Alta began to laugh.

Tata and Tabitha began to leave in a fit of rage.

"Father! Mother!" Alta called out and hurried after them. "How could you? Why would you try to do this to me? I thought you loved me."

"We do love you dear," Tabitha replied. "That is why we so desperately want you to leave that heretic so that you come back to the Church. Your soul's everlasting abode is more important than your temporal happiness."

"I know for sure that I am going to go to Heaven," Alta responded. "Do you know for sure that you will?"

"Your assurance is sin," replied Tabitha.

"No, it is biblical," John replied before Alta could. "I've read the Bible, you haven't. I know what it says, and God has opened my eyes to the truth of His wonderful salvation."

"Anyone can claim that God has opened their eyes to the truth," retorted Tata. "You are a heretic. I know you will burn in hell forever for leading my daughter and many others astray."

"You have a form of godliness but deny the power thereof," John responded.

Tata and Tabitha then stormed out of the chapel.

"I think their plan was to report our congregation to the bishop if the church tribunal declared your marriage to be void," Barzillai stated. "They certainly don't want you to be executed or even thrown in prison, so I don't think they will report us."

Alta began to weep and Jacobus hugged her. The rest gathered around them to try to console her.

After Easter that year, William returned to Normandy to display his triumphs, leaving his half-brother Odo, and a friend named William FitzOsbern in charge of Engla Land. The people of Engla Land hoped he would never come back. He took Edwin, Morcar, Edgar the Ætheling, and some other Anglo-Saxons along with him, much to their displeasure.

CHAPTER 12

PREPARATION FOR THE MISSION

Zebedee, take your sword and your shield to the market place tomorrow and use them to buy two thralls, the Lord said to Zebedee in a dream the next Friday night. *Ask Deborah and Barzillai if they would adopt them. Then free them.*

The next morning. Zebedee took his large sword and his large shield and went to the marketplace. He walked to where the thrall trading took place. There were several thegns trying to sell a thrall or two each, but two thralls in particular caught his attention, a young woman slightly younger and almost as beautiful as Cleena, bound with a chain around her neck, holding a baby less than a year old in her arms.

"Beautiful, isn't she?" asked the man holding the other end of the chain around the young woman's neck. "I was planning to take her to Bristol so she could be sold to someone from Ireland. I heard they pay better for thralls, especially for beautiful young women like this. Since I would rather not have to travel to Bristol and back, I wanted to see if someone in London might pay a higher price for her. Anyway, how much are you willing to pay for them?"

"What happened to your husband?" Zebedee asked the young woman, ignoring her owner.

She looked up and answered, "I don't have one."

She looked down again as a tear ran down her cheek.

"What happened to the father of your child?" Zebedee queried.

She simply pointed at her owner and began to weep.

Zebedee stared at her owner with incredulity. Then he became irate.

"What is wrong with you?" Zebedee yelled at the man.

"Who are you to judge me?" asked the young woman's owner. "Besides, she and her child are my property. I can do with them as I please. If you are not interested in buying them, just move along, man."

Zebedee clasped the hilt of his sword for a few moments, wanting to slay the man.

"Stop," said the owner of the two thralls.

Zebedee calmed himself and removed his scabbard with his sword still in it from his belt.

"I will give you this sword and this shield for them," Zebedee said to the man.

"What?" exclaimed the man in astonishment. He was familiar with swords which had gold rimmed handles. "Really?"

"Yes," Zebedee said.

"Alright, they are all yours, my friend," he said to Zebedee.

"What is your name?" Zebedee asked the young woman after purchasing her and her baby.

"Mary," she replied.

"What about your baby's name?" Zebedee asked.

"Benjamin," she replied.

"Do you believe in the Lord Jesus Christ?" Zebedee asked.

"No," she replied.

"Why not?" Zebedee questioned.

"Why would God let me go through all that I went through?" she said. "Why would He allow so much suffering and injustice to happen? And why did you purchase us with such a magnificent sword and magnificent shield?"

"We live in a fallen world," Zebedee explained to her. "When God created the world, there was no sin, suffering, or death, but Adam and Eve, the first two humans, disobeyed God. Through their first act of disobedience, sin, suffering, and death entered the world. Sin deserves everlasting suffering and death. Jesus came to save us from sin and its punishment. Last night, God spoke to me in a dream and told me to come here today and purchase two slaves with my sword and shield. God Almighty is my Lord and Master. I strive to obey Him."

"I'm sorry, I don't want to offend you, but it was just a dream," said the young woman.

"How do you know this seax on my belt was made by a bladesmith?" Zebedee asked her. "How do you know it didn't just suddenly come into existence?"

"What?" she laughed.

"Living creatures are a lot more complex than even the finest of swords," Zebedee said, "and you think the universe and life just suddenly came into existence?"

"Hmm," she said, introspectively.

"God has some pleasant surprises for you," Zebedee said to her. "He loves you more than you could imagine. He has seen your suffering and He has helped you."

For the first time, Zebedee saw her smile, which made Zebedee very happy and thankful.

Zebedee took her to Barzillai and Deborah's house. Only Deborah, Martha, and Harold were home. He explained Mary's and Benjamin's situation to Deborah in private.

"Would you adopt her if I free her?" Zebedee asked.

"Yes," Deborah responded. "Wait, I have to talk to Barzillai first. Let's go to the chapel."

After hearing the story of the woman and child, Barzillai said, "Of course we will adopt her and the child."

John, Barzillai, Deborah, Harold, and Martha accompanied Zebedee as he went to the city hall and freed Mary and Benjamin. Barzillai and Deborah then adopted Mary; she cried again, but this time with tears of joy.

"Last night I cried out to God in anger and asked Him to prove that He exists," Mary began. "I told Him I saw no reason to believe in or worship Him. I told Him I didn't want to go to a foreign land where I won't even understand the language. I asked Him to show me that He truly loved me and Benjamin. He heard my cry. He answered my prayer even though I don't deserve it. Maybe it was for Benjamin's sake."

"Grace is goodness we don't deserve," Barzillai explained. "None of us deserves anything but death and hell. God proved His love for us by sending His Son from Heaven to Earth, to live the perfect life, to die on the cross for our sins, and to rise from the grave, conquering death. Jesus Christ, the Son of God, then ascended back to Heaven and He will come again. God grants everlasting life to all those who believe in His Son."

"I believe," Mary replied as she continued crying joyfully.

When they went back to Barzillai's and Deborah's house, they found Lydia had returned from her errand, and was holding a baby who looked to be less than a month old, in her arms.

"I adopted her," she explained. "As I passed by a convent, I saw a woman around my age abandoning her at the front door. I named her Judith."

"I didn't think I would have any children," Deborah said, "but now I have seen four of my grandchildren."

"God is good," Barzillai exclaimed. "This baby will hear the true gospel."

Barzillai and Deborah held their newest grandchild in their arms.

"Would you like to carry her, Zebedee?" Deborah asked Zebedee.

"No, I'm afraid not," Zebedee said.

"Why not?" Deborah questioned.

"She looks like she is less than a month old," Zebedee answered, "which means she is still very delicate. I'm afraid of holding such delicate babies. What if I accidently hurt them?"

Everyone else inside the house laughed.

"It will be fine," Lydia said. "You just have to make sure you support her head and neck and be extra careful."

"I'm sorry," Zebedee responded. "I would rather not."

"Alright," Lydia laughed. "That is fine; there is no need to apologize."

"How much would that sword and shield have been worth?" Barzillai asked Zebedee a few minutes later.

"I don't know," answered Zebedee.

"I have to pay you back for them," said Barzillai.

"Not at all," Zebedee said.

"But I must," insisted Barzillai.

"I don't need a sword or a shield," Zebedee said. "I still have my seax. Besides, that sword and shield were too heavy for me anyway."

"Fine, then," said Barzillai, "but I would still like you to do something for me, and it will be very good for you, too."

"What is it?" Zebedee asked.

"As you know, your oldest brother John and I have been working on making another copy of the Bible," began Barzillai. "We have been working on it all day, seven days a week, with a few days off, for months now. I would like to spend more time with Deborah, our daughters, and their children. Can you please work with John and finish what I started? This is a great opportunity for you to read the Bible more and to study it better."

"I wish I could," Zebedee replied, honestly. "I really do, but I have to help my parents on their farm. They cannot afford to hire someone else to replace me."

"Is that it?" Barzillai questioned. "Any other obstacles or impediments?"

"No," replied Zebedee.

"Perfect," Barzillai said. "I will pay your parents to hire someone else so that you can do me this huge favor."

Zebedee beamed and chuckled briefly.

"So, what do you say?" queried Barzillai. "Do we have an agreement?"

"Yes," Zebedee responded. "Thank you very much, Barzillai."

Zebedee ran home to inform his parents, who were delighted. They found someone that very day to work on their farm instead of Zebedee, and he agreed to start the next Monday.

The next day, at the beginning of the church service, Barzillai announced, "I have some great news. Peter, our deacon, has finally agreed to serve as an overseer, with greater responsibilities of teaching and talking care of the flock, and Abraham has agreed to serve as a deacon, to assist us with counseling and serving the needs of the members."

"I know we need to drink beer, cider, or mead every day to quench our thirst and refresh us," Barzillai said while preaching. "But we should be very careful not to get drunk. We shouldn't even get close to what would be considered drunk. Not only does overdrinking harm one's health, it impairs one's judgment as well. This can cause someone to do something horrible which they would never do if they were in their right mind. And one may also be unaware of what is happening when they are very drunk, and not remember anything about it later."

The next day, Zebedee began working with John in the chapel.

"Don't copy Job, Psalms, Proverbs, Ecclesiastes, and Song of Solomon into that Old Testament codex," John instructed Zebedee. "If you do, some other books won't fit in that codex, but this New Testament codex will have enough space for them. I will copy them into this one and mark them as belonging to the Old Testament. In fact, I have finished making a copy of the New Testament, and I have already begun copying Job into this codex."

By early May, John finished copying the five poetic books into the codex with the New Testament.

"I'll copy the rest of the Old Testament," John told Zebedee, who had already copied a few books of the prophets. "Meanwhile, you should read the New Testament repeatedly."

In early August, John finished copying the rest of the Old Testament the same day that Zebedee finished perusing the New Testament for the seventh time.

"Now we need to spread the Word more," John told Zebedee.

"How?" Zebedee queried. "Whom should we tell?"

"Do you remember that couple in York, in whose house you, Clement and Thomas stayed?" John asked.

"Of course," said Zebedee. "I could never forget Adam and Eve."

"How can we not tell them?" John asked. "I have been praying about it for a while now. I think I should give these two new codices to Barzillai and take these large old ones to York with me. Our parents can always borrow codices and scrolls from the repository. I want to be a missionary, even if it is in my own country, and the people in York will almost see me as a foreigner anyway. Why don't you come with me? It will be very difficult to go on a mission alone, and it is good for a congregation to have more than one overseer."

"I would love to," Zebedee responded. "Before leaving York, I told them I would come see them again, and explain the wrong teachings of the Roman churches and the true teachings of the Bible. I have also been asking the Lord to make a way for me to go see them again. How long do you think we will stay in York?"

"I think we should move there," John replied.

"But, what about…?" Zebedee began.

"What about…?" asked John.

"I was going to say, 'What about Mother, Father, Jacobus, and all our friends here?'" Zebedee said. "But I remembered what Jesus said about leaving one's father, mother, sisters, and brothers to follow Him."

John smiled and said, "I think we should leave after you finish reading the Old Testament twice and then read the New Testament again. Don't just read it in a hurry without trying to understand what you read. You should always try to understand what you are reading and ask the Holy Spirit to guide you. But don't take too long, travelling all the way to Yorkshire in the winter is now more perilous than ever. We are not even allowed to gather wood to make a fire in many areas, so if you don't finish reading in time, we will have to wait until spring next year to go there."

"When should we tell the others about our plan?" Zebedee questioned.

"I think we should tell Father, Mother, and Barzillai today," John answered. "I think Barzillai will make an announcement at the right time."

"That sounds reasonable," replied Zebedee.

They told their parents about their plans that day. Simon and Priscilla had mixed feelings about it. The following day, they informed Barzillai and his family about their plans of moving to York. Barzillai and Deborah had mixed emotions about it, too, whereas Lydia and Mary were mostly excited about the mission, and Harold and Martha were very unhappy about Zebedee leaving, as he played with them frequently.

"I knew that God would use the two of you mightily," Barzillai told John and Zebedee. "I had hoped that you two would become the next overseers of our congregation. I am old and Peter is catching up."

"It doesn't feel fair," said Deborah, "but God's plans are far better than ours, and He will provide for His sheep."

The following Sunday, Barzillai announced, "John, Zebedee, and I have finished making another Englisc copy of the Bible. John and Zebedee will continue to study the Bible from these large codices till early or mid-November, after which they plan to go to York as missionaries. Please continue to uphold them in your prayers. We normally don't collect tithes and offerings because we haven't sent out missionaries in decades. We individually help those in our congregation who are in need, and we give to the poor individually as we are led by the Lord, but now, if anyone would like to make a contribution to help support them in their work, you can do so. There is no hurry, you have time till they leave."

That Sunday, Barzillai preached about why God allows His children to suffer apart from disciplining them. Some of the reasons Barzillai mentioned were: to teach them something; to prevent them from becoming proud; to build their character and perseverance; to make them more dependent upon Him; to prevent greater suffering, and to help them understand other people's suffering so that they can reach out to help them more effectively.

By early November, Zebedee finished reading the Old Testament twice, and then the New Testament once more, while John worked on memorizing the Gospel of John and some of Paul's epistles in Englisc, which he did successfully by then. Zebedee and John spent a couple days discussing the Scriptures which each other and learning from each other.

The only ones who cried when John and Zebedee said their goodbyes in mid-November were Zebedee, Priscilla, Simon, Barzillai, Deborah, Harold, and Martha. Some were either so excited about the mission that their joy was greater than their sorrow, while others just did not express their sorrow, and still others were too caught up with their own affairs to be bothered about it.

"Please continue to pray for us," John requested of the congregation. "We need God to direct us and strengthen us every step of the way."

Abraham gave them a bag of silver shillings and pennies from the congregation, saying, "Every household in the congregation contributed."

Barzillai gave Zebedee and John two horses and a wagon, two barrels, and a large blanket to cover the wagon.

"My final gifts to you two before you leave," Barzillai told them. "You can hide the codices in the barrels and cover the barrels with your spare clothes. Feel free to sell these gifts once you have no more use for them."

"Thank you very much, everyone," Zebedee and John said together.

"I highly recommend that you buy two barrels of beer now to take with you on your journey so you don't become weak and too thirsty," Barzillai told them.

CHAPTER 13

THE MISSION IN YORKSHIRE

Zebedee and John arrived in York late in November, just before the beginning of winter. Zebedee found Adam and Eve's house fairly easily. John, who had never seen the outside of their house, followed Zebedee's lead.

"I hope they still live here," Zebedee said to John as he got down from the wagon.

"Yes," said John. "If they don't, ask the current residents of the house if they know where Adam and Eve are now. I'll wait here in the wagon."

"All right," Zebedee replied.

Zebedee knocked on the door with excitement and anticipation.

Adam opened the door. When he saw Zebedee at the door and John in a wagon several feet behind him his jaw dropped and his eyes sparkled.

"Hello, Adam," Zebedee said. "It is very nice to see you again."

"Eve, they are back," Adam turned around and exclaimed loudly. "They have finally come back."

"Who's back, dear?" Eve asked.

"Zebedee and John," Adam responded.

"What?" Eve exclaimed and hurried to the door.

"We have been praying that you would come to our house again and tell us what the Bible really teaches." Adam exclaimed after Eve came to stand beside him. "We were beginning to think you had forgotten about us."

"I could never forget your hospitality," Zebedee replied. "I had been praying about coming back to York to see you and tell you the truth about what the Bible says. I asked the Lord to make a way for me to do so, but the credit of making the decision goes to John, not me."

"Please come in," Eve said. "I've almost finished preparing our evening meal."

"Is there a place we can keep our wagon and horses?" Zebedee inquired.

"In our stable," Adam replied. "I will show you where it is. It is just outside the city."

"Thank you," Zebedee responded.

"Be back soon," Eve said to Adam.

After the horses started trotting, John said, "Why don't we sell the horses and wagon tomorrow? I doubt we will need them again!"

"Aren't we going to visit London again?" Zebedee asked.

"Yea, but we won't need to take these codices with us," John answered.

"Wait, so you are moving to York?" Adam asked in shock.

"Yes," Zebedee and John smiled and replied simultaneously.

"So there are codices hidden in the wagon?" Adam inquired.

"That's right," John replied. "There are two barrels under the blanket, and each contains a large codex."

"What's so special about these codices?" asked Adam.

"They contain a copy of the Bible, in Englisċ," Zebedee answered.

"What?" Adam exclaimed with surprise and joy.

"Why do you think it took us so long to come here?" John asked and chuckled.

Adam laughed with joy.

"Although, these are an older copy, not the one we worked on," Zebedee said.

"Why didn't you bring the newer copy?" Adam questioned.

"So that you know that I am not making anything up," John clarified.

Oh, Zebedee thought to himself. *I thought he just wanted to leave a newer copy with the congregation in London because it would last longer. I cannot believe how dumb I am.*

"I know a very rich thegn who might be willing to buy the horses and the wagon, and he lives close by; we can go to him today," Adam said.

Adam directed them to a large house. He and Zebedee got down from the wagon after it stopped, and Adam knocked on the door.

"Hello, Bada," Adam said to the man who opened the door. "This is Zebedee, the hero of the battle at Stamford Bridge, and that is his brother John in the wagon. John was the monk who suddenly appeared in my house and then disappeared after God brought Thomas back to life and healed Zebedee. They would like to sell their horses and their wagon. Would you be interested in buying them?"

"Surely," Bada replied. "It is a pleasure to finally meet you. I'm glad you've come back to visit York."

"Actually..." Zebedee and Adam both began.

"We are moving here," Zebedee finished.

"What?" exclaimed Bada. "Wonderful."

"Now, I would like to know how the Western Church and the Eastern Church are not following the Bible," Bada said after he gave John and Zebedee some gold in exchange for the horses and the wagon.

"They will tell you tomorrow, my friend," Adam said. "Eve is waiting for us."

"Alright," replied Bada. "I can't wait."

Bada and his oldest son Cyneheard drove the horses and wagon to Bada's stable outside the city and returned to their place of residence while John, Zebedee, and Adam walked back to Adam and Eve's house with their belongings and the codices in the barrels. After dinner, John explained to Adam and Eve how the Roman churches were not following the Bible and proved it by showing them passages in the Bible. After that Zebedee informed them about the congregation in London.

Adam and Eve were filled with wonder and amazement by the great love of God.

The next morning, Bada and his family came to Adam's and Eve's house and found the answers they sought.

"So what are you going to do now?" Adam asked John and Zebedee.

"I think we should seek to buy a hut," John replied.

"Why?" Adam asked. "You can stay with Eve and me. We have lots of space since our son Paul moved out with his wife five years ago."

"We didn't want him to leave," Eve said, "but he and his wife wanted to."

"Thank you very much for your hospitality," John responded, "but we don't want to be a bother to anyone."

"Please," said Eve. "It is no bother."

"If Adam and Eve are bothering you, you are welcome to stay at my house," Bada said, causing ripples of laughter in the room. "Although I should warn you, it is more crowded."

"Thank you Adam, Eve, Bada," John said, feeling very grateful, while at the same time not wanting to inconvenience either Bada's family or Adam's family. "Zebedee and I will talk about it."

"Why do you want to waste your money on a house, even a small one?" Adam questioned. "You can put it to much better use."

"How?" John and Zebedee asked at the same time.

"By buying thousands of single sheets of parchment and lots of ink," Adam answered.

"What?" asked John, confused. "Single sheets? For what purpose?"

"Write on each sheet a letter listing the most erroneous teachings of the Eastern and Western Roman churches, urging the readers to leave them and to follow the true Gospel of Jesus Christ," Adam explained. "Eve and I were talking about it yesterday. We hope you can send one copy of the letter to every household in York, or better yet, all of Yorkshire."

"That's a great idea," Bada exclaimed. "I'm sure we would all like to see the eyes of everyone in Yorkshire open to the truth of Scripture."

"And God certainly wants that more than we do," Zebedee said.

"I'm not sure we have quite enough money for that," John said, "but we can certainly send a copy to all the houses in the city. We should exercise caution, however, until sufficient copies are made, and then quickly distribute them all over the city. The Western Roman Church will surely persecute us, but not before we have accomplished our mission."

"I would be happy to give money for the Lord's service," Bada said, "but we will need many hands to distribute all those letters. I think we should start by informing our relatives and friends about what the Bible really teaches."

"Yes, of course," Adam replied. "It will take time to write all those letters anyway."

"Why don't you inform all those you can, today," John suggested to Adam, Eve, and Bada. "For now, I think you should just call those whom you know will not report us to the Western Roman Church clergy or any other governing authorities. Call those whom you can trust. Ask them to come here tomorrow evening, after their meal, if that is all right with you."

"That's fine," Adam and Eve responded. "They are welcome in our house."

"Alright, let's go," said Bada, as they all hurried away.

The next evening, people started coming to Adam and Eve's house before Adam, Eve, John and Zebedee finished their own meal.

"Oh my," Eve exclaimed to the first set of visitors, who happened to be good friends of theirs and Bada's. "You came earlier than I expected."

"We did not want to miss anything, so we came as soon as we finished eating," one of them replied. "Please continue your meal, though, don't mind us."

The house was crowded with people very soon.

John preached to them about the major errors of the Roman churches and about what the Bible really says about those matters. He read to them from the Bible to prove what he was saying was true. He then informed them about the congregation in southern Engla Land, without specifying the city or what kind of abandoned building they gathered in, for their safety in case anyone listening decided to report them. Everyone listened intently and marveled at what they learned.

"We can meet here on Sundays," Adam announced. "John and Zebedee will be the overseers and pastors. Bada and I will be the deacons to serve you. Some of you can come in the morning and some of you can come in the afternoon. For now, please don't tell anyone unless you are sure that they won't turn us over to the authorities."

They had two church services every Sunday. John and Zebedee discussed with each other what they would preach on Sundays and John preached more often than Zebedee.

John, Zebedee, Adam, Eve, Bada and anyone else who wanted to study the Bible gathered at Adam's and Eve's house the other six days of the week for Bible studies lead by John or Zebedee. Their numbers increased gradually. Eventually, they had to hold two church services on Saturdays as well, and two Bible studies all other days of the week.

In their free time, John, Zebedee, Adam, and Bada were making copies of the letter which John wrote to send to all the households in York and the surrounding regions. John, Zebedee, and Adam made copies in Adam and Eve's house while Bada made copies in his own house. They did not buy all the sheets of parchment or all the ink from the same store to avoid raising any suspicion.

The contents of the letter read:

Dear citizens of Engla Land,

Greetings.

I was a monk. While studying the Bible at a monastery, I discovered that neither the Eastern Church nor the Western Church was following the Bible. There are hundreds, maybe thousands, of Christians on Earth who are part of neither church, whose beliefs are far more biblical, and I am now one of those Christians.

Praying to anyone apart from God Himself is unbiblical. It is sin!

All believers are saved by God's grace alone and through our faith in Christ alone, not by any works or sacraments. Jesus Christ suffered the full punishment for all our sins on the cross. God wants us to obey Him out of love for Him, not because we are afraid of

177

being thrown in the lake of fire. He empowers us to love and serve Him as we grow in our faith.

Water baptism doesn't save you. The Holy Spirit indwells you once you place your faith in Christ. That is when you are saved.

The bread and wine which we partake during communion only symbolize Jesus Christ's body and blood, they do not actually become His body and His blood. Holy communion is not a sacrifice. Christ died once for all and He is now alive forevermore.

The pope is neither the head of the Church nor the vicar of Christ, and neither he nor the Apostle Peter are the Rock on which Christ built the Church. The Lord Jesus Christ Himself is the Rock; our God is our only Rock.

Finally, there is nothing special about Latin. Church services should be held entirely in the language that the congregation understands, which of course means the Bible needs to be translated into that language so it can be read in that language. The pope, cardinals, and bishops do not want you to know what the Bible really teaches because they want to control you.

I urge you to leave the apostate Roman Church. The true Church of God is not a visible organization, it is made up of all true believers in Heaven and on Earth.

Sincerely,

John,

An ardent student of the Bible.

The following year, 1068, Edwin and Morcar returned to Engla Land and commenced an insurgence against William with support from Gospatric, the new eorl of Northumbria. Morcar sent letters and messengers throughout much of Engla Land to rally more supporters. He campaigned extensively in York. To quell the uprising, King William returned to Engla Land with his army and built a wooden castle in Warwick. Edwin and Morcar surrendered not long afterwards. William built more castles in Engla Land, including one in York, before returning to Normandy.

Early in November that year, when Adam, Eve, Bada, John, and Zebedee were alone in Adam's and Eve's house, Adam said to John and Zebedee,

"John, Zebedee, you should visit your family and friends in London. You should celebrate Christmas with your family this year. Why don't you spend the winter in London? We will watch over things here while you are away."

"That sounds great," John replied. "Thank you very much."

"Yes," Zebedee said. "Thank you."

"Don't mention it," Adam responded. "It is the least we can do after all you have done."

"You have already done so much," Zebedee replied.

"I don't know what we would have done without you three," John said.

John and Zebedee left York in mid-November and arrived in London near the end of November. Bada had let them borrow the horses they sold him.

Clement and Cleena were now married to each other, and Eva was married to a young man named Abel, who had been a member of Barzillai's congregation before Zebedee found them.

Mary was engaged to Ælfsige, who still worked on Jacobus' farm, and Lydia was engaged to Dermont.

Barzillai and Deborah were not happy about both their daughters and their daughters' children leaving them so soon, but to their utter delight, Ælfsige and Mary asked to stay with them.

"Look at it this way," Deborah said to her husband. "We have daughters and grandchildren, and soon, God willing, we will also have sons."

"You are right," Barzillai responded, and laughed. "And we will still see Lydia, Martha, Harold, and Judith often."

John and Zebedee reported to the congregation in London how God had blessed their work in York and were delighted to learn that the entire congregation was going to celebrate Christmas together.

"What made you change your mind?" Zebedee asked Barzillai.

"Since we are not celebrating them as rituals or attributing any spiritual significance to the days, but celebrating them as informal, joyful commemorations, I think it is fine to celebrate Christmas and Easter," Barzillai explained.

The entire congregation rejoiced at the report of the mission in York.

In January the next year, 1069, Edgar the Ætheling became the leader of an insurrection against King William started by the Northumbrians and took control of Northumbria. William returned to Engla Land, crushed the rebellion at York, punished the residents of York by letting his troops plunder them, and built another castle there. Edgar and the other leaders of the rebellion escaped before they could be punished.

On the last Sunday of February 1069, John and Zebedee informed the congregation in London about their plan to distribute the copies of John's letter. Upon hearing this, the congregation in London became very worried.

"That is very risky," Barzillai told them. "It could either be a great success with too many converts to persecute, or it could lead to all your deaths. I don't see any other possibilities."

"I know you have spent a lot of time, money, and effort on this plan, but I don't think you should carry it out," Priscilla said. "Please stop it immediately upon your return."

"It wasn't our idea," John replied, "and if those who had the idea are willing to take the risk, how can we not?"

"We believe God wants us to do this," Zebedee said.

"Remember what Jesus said," John began and quoted the passage corresponding to Matthew 16:25, where Jesus says, "For whoever wishes to save his life shall lose it; but whoever loses his life for My sake shall find it."

"But that doesn't mean you should just throw your life away pointlessly," Simon responded. "You are doing good work there, just keep doing that. Forget about distributing the copies of the letter. Just burn them before the authorities or the Roman Church clergy find them."

"No!" John and Zebedee responded adamantly.

"Your actions may start a new wave of persecution that will come to us as well," Deborah said.

John and Zebedee frowned. The thought had occurred to both of them but they believed it was unlikely and convinced themselves that it would not happen.

"Maybe you all should leave Engla Land," John said after a long pause.

"What?" many of the congregants exclaimed.

"That is a big move," Barzillai said. "All of us? A very big move."

"Maybe you should leave if you hear of persecution in Yorkshire," Zebedee replied. "It should be safe here till then."

"I don't want to be the only child," Jacobus cried as he hugged his brothers.

The entire congregation wept as John and Zebedee departed from London to go back to York in early March 1069, wondering if the next time they saw them would be in Heaven.

Thank you, Lord, thank you for giving me the gift of celibacy, Zebedee prayed silently as they began their journey back to York. *You used me to save Martha and Harold's lives, You used me to free Mary and Benjamin, and You have kept me from becoming a husband and father so I can now unhesitatingly lay down my life for the sake of the Gospel.*

They were back in York in mid-March.

On the morning of Saturday, May 23, the congregation in York began distributing the five thousand copies of John's letter to every house in York and to many in the surrounding villages. Almost all of Yorkshire was in a tumult. They finished distributing every letter before evening, but an hour before the last letter was distributed, on the urging of the priests in York, four of the men who were distributing letters were captured by the authorities.

"The priests are calling all the residents of York to come to the town square!" was repeatedly proclaimed loudly by multiple announcers stationed throughout the city.

Two of the men captured were brothers in their twenties. The other two were father and son; the son was in his late teens.

"You all know by now about the anti-Church tracts being handed out by some heretics." announced a priest. "These men were among the distributers. Young men sometimes don't know how to use their energy, so they will leave with a mere fifteen lashes each, but that older man will be burned alive at the stake, both as punishment for trying to lead people astray from the truth and as a warning for others not to do what he did."

The older man's wife and other children fought back their tears with all their might so as not to get caught.

"Wait!" shouted John. "What will that accomplish? Do you really think this will change anyone's mind?"

"What do you propose?" the priest asked John.

"Hold a public debate or discussion in the city hall with the overseers of this group," John said. "Wouldn't proving them wrong by quoting the Bible put an end to this movement?"

"But there is no Englisċ translation of the Bible and most of the laity don't understand Latin," the priest replied.

John trembled a little, unsure what to say, then said, "I memorized parts of an Englisċ translation of the New Testament, in a different city. As long as you pick priests who are well versed in Latin and can translate from Englisċ to Latin it will be absolutely fine. The laity will hear what the Bible says in Englisċ."

"Which city has an Englisċ translation of the Bible?" the priest asked. "Why do they have an Englisċ translation?"

"Why does it matter?" John asked.

"Wait, so you are one of them, aren't you?" said the priest. "Wait, no, you must be their leader."

"The heretics will quote passages out of context and confuse the laity," the priest said to the crowd. "And they may use cunning words to sway weak minds."

"You can read the context of the passage for yourself in Latin if you think I omitted something important during the debate," John shouted. "Show the people of York the truth. Delay the punishments till our group has been proved heretical to the residents of York."

"Fine," the priest said. "They will be left unpunished for now."

Another priest came close to the first priest and whispered something to him.

The first priest then announced, "We challenge the heretics to send their two best debaters to the city hall to debate us two Saturdays from today, after the noontime meal."

Zebedee was John's partner in the debate on Saturday, June 6.

The city hall was surrounded by armed guards on that sunny day and was more crowded than it had ever been, with Normans, Anglo-Saxon thegns, and Anglo-Saxon ceorls inside.

John and Zebedee did very well in the debate against the two priests, whose names were Solomon and Timothy, however, only about half of the listeners were convinced. The debaters did not know who was convinced. The priests of the Roman Church, who knew that the Church of Rome was proved wrong, and that those with an open mind would have realized it, were furious.

"Arrest the heretics!" Timothy shouted.

"Wait!" cried a Norman nobleman.

"Leave them alone!" shouted someone else in the audience.

"They were right!" shouted another.

"They won the debate!" shouted yet another.

"Silence!" shouted Solomon. "They will be burned alive. That will just be a taste of the everlasting hellfire where all heretics will end up."

William Malet, high shire reeve of Yorkshire, accompanied by some other Norman nobles, strode to the front of the hall in front of John and Zebedee, turned around to face the audience, and said, "These men and all who are with them are under my protection now."

"What?" exclaimed Solomon and Timothy.

"Where do you gather to worship?" he asked John and Zebedee.

"In a house," Zebedee answered.

John did not answer because he was worried that this might be a trick to find the others.

"Well, now that there will be more of you, I think you should gather here at the city hall on Sundays," Malet responded. "I don't believe your new teachings, but some of my friends here do."

"Thank you, sir," Zebedee exclaimed.

John sighed in relief and said, "Yes, thank you very much."

Cheers erupted from the audience.

John and Zebedee had to hold three meetings on Sundays at the city hall instead of at Adam's and Eve's house because of all the people coming to attend, not only from York, but also from some of the surrounding villages. News of this began to spread all over Yorkshire, and soon the city hall was packed and overflowing during all three meetings.

The priests of the Roman churches in York were vexed with the growth of the Bible believing Christians and the decline in the number of people attending their churches, but due to William Malet's friendship with King William, their hands were tied.

Mondays through Saturdays, John lead a daily Bible study at Bada's house, while Zebedee lead one each day at Adam's and Eve's house.

One fine Sunday afternoon in July, a man approached John and Zebedee after the second service and said, "Greetings, brothers. My name is Jedidiah. Word about you two and your work here in York has spread throughout Yorkshire. I attend a similar congregation in a village somewhere in Yorkshire. How is the congregation down south?"

"They are doing well," Zebedee exclaimed joyfully.

"Thank you so much for coming," said John. "It is very encouraging to hear about other congregations of Bible believing Christians."

"We should be thanking you," Jedidiah responded. "We have been edified by your courage and boldness."

Jedidiah stayed in Bada's house for a few days before returning to his village.

There was great joy in York as John and Zebedee's ministry was very fruitful.

CHAPTER 14

THE EMIGRATION FOLLOWING THE HARROWING EVENTS

In August, Edgar the Ætheling lead another insurrection against William, and this time with a new ally, Sweyn, king of Denmark. They captured York, stormed the Norman castles in the city, and killed all the Normans in it except William and Hesilia Malet, their daughter, and one of their sons, who were all taken hostage.

Meanwhile, there were two uprisings against King William in the south.

Many in Yorkshire and the surrounding regions proclaimed that Edgar was their king. Many ceorls hoped that Edgar would reverse the policies that William introduced that made their lives harder. The Anglo-Saxon clergy also supported Edgar.

The city hall could no longer be used for church meetings, so those who used to gather at the city hall began to gather at Adam's house and Bada's house on multiple days to accommodate everyone.

The Anglo-Saxon clergymen convinced Edgar to kill the people whom they labelled heretics. Edgar sent troops to Adam's and Eve's house and to Bada's house while Bible studies were being held to kill all those gathered in those houses. John, Zebedee, Adam, Eve, Adam and Eve's son, Paul and his entire family, and Bada and his entire family, were among those slain. All of them were ecstatic as they faced the sword, knowing that they would see their Savior, Whom they loved more than life itself.

The codices containing the Englisċ translation of the Bible were burned. The whole city was called to the city square and given the news. Weeping and

186

loud wailing erupted throughout the crowd along with shouts of, "Murderers!"

"Apostates, come back to the Church of Rome," Timothy announced. "Confess your sins to a priest and God will forgive you."

When news of the rebellions reached King William in Normandy, he flew into a fit of rage.

"How many times must I forgive these stupid, ungrateful Anglo-Saxons?" William shouted. "These Anglo-Saxons, and especially that young fellow Edgar, are taking advantage of my mercy. And this time they have massacred many of my Norman nobles. Unforgivable. This time I will not show any mercy, I will show them my wrath and my vengeance. Engla Land will loathe me, but they will fear me. If I have to kill thousands of innocent Anglo-Saxons to make sure I punish all the guilty and teach the people of Engla Land a lesson, then so be it."

"You would have the blessings of the bishop of Rome if only he knew of the situation," replied one of King William's royal chaplains. "Do as you have said."

"What?" exclaimed William and the rest of his royal advisors together in utter astonishment.

"I have just been notified by a report that there is now a large group of re-baptizing heretics in Yorkshire and that they are growing," the chaplain explained.

"Re-baptizing heretics?" rang the voice of one of the king's royal advisors.

"I have heard of them, these re-baptizing heretics," said the king. "They are heretics that the Church of Rome has been trying to wipe out for hundreds of years now. Based on what I heard, I had thought they had all been exterminated before my time, or at least that any survivors would have learned their lesson. Clearly this shows us that sometimes we must kill innocent people to make sure we kill all the guilty."

"Agreed," responded the royal chaplain.

After returning to Engla Land and vanquishing the rebels along the border of the land of the Welsh and the Welsh kings supporting them, William and his troops headed north to Yorkshire. Once they reached the

River Aire, William ordered his army to burn all the farms and houses they encountered along the way to York, which they did.

King William and his army arrived at York a few days before Christmas, but when they did, they discovered that the rebels had gone into hiding. The Danes made a tactical retreat to their ships which were in the Humber Estuary, and the Anglo-Saxon rebels tactically retreated to some forests and hills after Edgar fled to Scotland.

Enraged, William ordered his army to set fire to many houses and other buildings in York as punishment for supporting Edgar's rebellion, but not before the four surviving Malets were rescued.

On Christmas Day, while wearing his crown, King William looked at the destruction his army caused with satisfaction and then marched them to meet the Danes at their ships. After reaching the coast where the Danes and their ships were stationed, William offered to pay them a large sum of silver and gold if they agreed to not engage his army in battle, but to leave Engla Land early in the spring of the upcoming year. The Danes agreed.

On January 1, 1070, King William divided his troops and ordered them to slaughter all the inhabitants of all the villages from the Humber Estuary to the River Tees, to plunder whatever they wanted, and to burn all that land to starve the rebels. His army did so. Tens of thousands of Anglo-Saxons were put to death via sword or spear or the fires. The massacres ended in April. About a hundred thousand Anglo-Saxons died soon after, because of the resulting famine.

Only two families who were a part of the congregation which John and Zebedee led in York managed to survive by escaping to Pictland, which later became part of Scotland.

When the congregation in London heard about the devastation of the north while it was still ongoing, they knew that John and Zebedee must have died. They all mourned for John and Zebedee. Simon and Priscilla finally understood some reasons God told Zebedee not to get married.

"We all need to ask the Lord for guidance," Barzillai said to the congregation on Sunday, March 14, 1070. "What should we do? Should we leave Engla Land? Where should we move to if we do? If you can fast and pray, please do so."

Two weeks later they had a vote and the vast majority voted to leave Engla Land and go to Normandy. So they all sold their property and moved to Normandy in June. The old chapel in London collapsed days later.

In Normandy, all of them either purchased or built houses close to each other so they could live in the same community. They did not preach to others till they learned the Norman language, and they only preached to friends whom they knew would not report them to any authorities or the clergy of the Western Roman Church.

Due to the destruction carried out by William's troops, a large portion of northern Engla Land became a wasteland for years. Many villages were uninhabited, and a great deal of farmland could not be cultivated for several years.

In August 1070, Lanfranc became the archbishop of Canterbury and Thomas of Bayeux, who had been one of Lanfranc's students, became the archbishop of York in December of the same year. Lanfranc was responsible for multiple changes in Engla Land. He worked toward mandating celibacy for priests, as not all priests in Engla Land were celibate at that time. A notable reform of his was convincing King William to prohibit the people of Engla Land from selling their thralls to people in other countries. Slavery had already been abolished in Normandy earlier in that century.

In the year 1073, Pope Alexander II forbade marriage between a man and a woman as distantly related as sixth cousins by changing the way the Western Roman Church measured degrees of kinship. It was sometimes hard to keep track of how distantly two people were related, so more marriages were "annulled" with forged documents indicating that a married couple was within the forbidden degrees of kinship. Of course, couples could pay the pope to grant them an exception, which often happened, since many nobles couldn't find other nobles in their country who were more distantly related to them than sixth cousins.

That same year, Jacobus said to Alta, "Alta, maybe we should stop praying for natural children and just adopt, like Barzillai and Deborah did. They had been praying for natural children for decades.

"Jacobus," exclaimed Alta joyfully, her eyes tearing up. "I'm pregnant!"

In the year 1080, when Cleena realized that she had become pregnant for the fifth time, she rejoiced like the previous four times, however, when she informed her husband, he feigned a smile and said, "Hooray!" He began to sob when she wasn't there, thinking how difficult it was to take care of all of them.

Clement then reminded himself that the Bible says that children are a gift from God and that God would empower him to take care of this child as well.

Cleena had a miscarriage when pregnant with their sixth child. Both Cleena and Clement wept, even though Clement did not want any more children. Cleena was informed by a physician, who was educated in Montpellier but had moved to Normandy, that if she became pregnant again she might die. Cleena wept bitterly.

"We still have five children," Clement said to his wife. "Why do you want more?"

"I wanted at least seven," she replied.

Clement decided not to tell her he had hoped they would not have any more after they had their third child. He hugged her, kissed her, and said, "It is all right. God only gives good gifts to His children."

At that time, King William's first castles in Engla Land were made of wood, but he later began building stone castles.

That decade, many of the congregants moved to other places to tell people about what the Bible really taught. Most just moved to other regions of France, some of them, such as Lydia's son Harold and his wife Hannah, went to Jerusalem as missionaries in the year 1086.

William, duke of Normandy and king of Engla Land, died on September 9, 1087. He was not shown much love or respect from his deathbed to his funeral. In his will, he left the duchy of Normandy to his oldest son, Robert, who had tried to usurp his father's position as duke of Normandy more than once. The king left Engla Land to William, his second oldest son who was still alive, and a large sum of money to his youngest son, Henry. He also bequeathed some of his possessions to Western Roman churches and some money to the poor. Robert succeeded his father as duke of Normandy and

William succeeded his father as king of Engla Land. The two went to war soon afterwards to gain control over the other's territory.

Epilogue

The Western Roman Church began giving plenary indulgences in the year 1095 when Pope Urban II called for the first crusade to free Jerusalem from Saracen control. He proclaimed at the Council of Clermont that he would grant a complete remission of all penance to those who participated in the crusades if they confessed their sins to a clergyman.

King William II died in a hunting accident in the year 1100 and was succeeded by his brother Henry as king of Engla Land.

In the year 1102, Anslem, archbishop of Canterbury, convened a Western Roman Church council in London. This council led to some changes in the Western Roman Church in England. Celibacy was mandated for clerics, monks, and nuns, while drunkenness was prohibited. Thralldom was denounced; all thralls were freed before the beginning of the next century. Thralldom was replaced by serfdom, which was not nearly as bad.

Seeing the power of the Welsh war bows, Engla Land began making similar war bows, which had heavy draw weights and could shoot sharp, steel tipped arrows with enough force to easily penetrate chain mail armor. As a result, Engla Land's armies eventually included thousands of archers.

Near the end of the 12th Century, some of the descendants of the Bible believing Christians in this story fellowshipped with Peter Waldo and the Waldensians after the latter were excommunicated from the Western Roman Church. Peter Waldo was a wealthy clothes merchant who paid some monks to translate the New Testament into the vernacular for him around 1170 AD. Upon perusing the New Testament, he discovered many of the false teachings of the Roman churches and started preaching in the streets of France.

Looking at the example of the Waldensians, they began to preach to others more boldly. Because of the beliefs these Christians shared with the Waldensians that contradicted the teachings of the Roman churches, they were also labeled Waldensians. The Waldensians also believed that the church of Rome was "Babylon the great, the mother of harlots and of abominations of the earth."

In letter to the bishop of Metz in 1199, Pope Innocent III condemned street preaching and lay people preaching, and he also condemned Bible studies which were not led by clergymen and were not inside Roman churches.

As time went on, the Norman culture influenced the Anglo-Saxon culture more and more. Everything from social classes and buildings to the language of the Anglo-Saxons, which we now call Englisċ or Old English, was transformed. For example, "huscarl" was changed to "housecarl", the spelling of "eorl" was changed to "earl", and the title "shire reeve" was changed to "sheriff". Names were not spared. The name Ealdgyth was eventually changed to Edith. The name Hreodbeorht was changed to Robert as they are cognates; and the name Jacobus was changed to James, instead of being shortened to Jacob, even though they are merely different forms of the same name. Some names were barely changed; for example, Osbeorn was changed to Osborn, Ælfgar was changed to Algar, and Ælfræd was changed to Alfred. Surnames were eventually introduced to Engla Land. Scandinavians who had participated in maritime activities in the past were eventually referred to as Vikings. Harald Sigurdsson is often called the last great Viking king. European soldiers who fought on horseback came to be known as knights; over time, knights and their horses became more heavily and better armored, which required the use of sharper weapons to counter. Gradually, Engla Land's wooden buildings were replaced by buildings of stone.

In 1215, at the Fourth Lateran Council, Pope Innocent III decreased the number of forbidden degrees of kinship pertaining to marriage to four, which does not extend past third cousins.

In the year 1229, at the Council of Toulouse, the Western Roman Church forbid the laity from possessing any passages of Scripture in their vernacular language, whereas in the past it was merely discouraged. The laity were not even allowed to have Latin copies of passages of Scripture with the exception of the Scripture contained in these three devotional books: *The Breviary*, which the clergy prayed, the *Psalter*, or *Book of Psalms and some litany*, and the *Little Office of the Blessed Virgin Mary*, which is a liturgy performed in honor of Mary.

In the year 1234, at the second Council of Tarragona, it was once again proclaimed to be impermissible for the laity to possess books of the Bible in their local language; all who did possess any had to hand them over to a bishop within eight days for them to be burned if they did not want to be treated as heretics.

For hundreds of years, the Western Roman Church, which is now called the Roman Catholic Church, extensively persecuted all those labelled as Waldensians; many were burned alive. Some who were wrongly labeled Waldensians fellowshipped with John Wycliffe and the Lollards in the 14th Century and some with Jan Hus and the Hussites in the 15th Century. The Hussites are now called Moravians.

John Wycliffe oversaw the first complete translation of the Bible into Middle English; he translated the Bible from the Latin Vulgate, not from the original languages. Although his translation included apocryphal books, he knew that they were not inspired by the Holy Spirit. The Roman Catholic Church and the Eastern Orthodox Church would not have considered the translation which Barzillai possessed a complete translation because it did not include the Apocrypha.

During Martin Luther's time, Roman Catholic letters of indulgences used to be handed out for both the dead and the living and could be obtained in many ways, including by giving money to the Roman Catholic Church. In his Ninety-five Theses, Martin Luther spoke against indulgences and implied that Christians should follow the Bible, even if the teachings of the Roman Catholic Church contradicted the Bible.

The reformers Martin Luther, John Calvin, and John Knox also believed that the Roman Catholic Church was "Babylon the great, the mother of harlots and of abominations of the earth."

Many Waldensians began to fellowship with the Reformers, joined a Protestant church, and adopted the practice of infant baptism in that century. The descendants of the Bible believing Christians in this story, who were falsely labelled "Waldensians," had been wiped out.

Later that century, Cardinal Stanislaus Hosius admitted that the Roman Catholic Church had been killing various groups whom it called Anabaptists for twelve centuries and declared Anabaptists to be worse heretics than the Lutherans and Zwinglians because they "re-baptize" believers who were baptized by a Roman Catholic priest.

Decades after William Tyndale and Myles Coverdale's translation of the Bible into English from Hebrew and Greek was completed in 1535, the Roman Catholic Church finally authorized an English translation of the Bible from the Latin Vulgate to save face. That translation is now called the Douay-Rheims Bible. The New Testament translation of the Douay-Rheims Bible was published in 1582 with a lot of comments while part of the Old Testament translation was published in 1609 and the remainder in 1610.

A privateer named John Hawkins restarted the English slave trade in the 16th Century. Slavery was abolished throughout the British Empire in the 19th Century.

In the 20th Century, the Roman Catholic church began allowing marriage between couples more distantly related than second cousins, and then first cousins.

Today the Bible is by far the bestselling book of all time. So far, the entire Bible has been translated into at least 724 languages, and the entire New Testament has been translated into over 2300 languages.

Unfortunately, many Christians today have no idea how wonderful the Holy Bible is and how much wisdom they could gain by studying it.

Sources

1. https://blog.tms.edu/when-did-praying-to-saints-start
2. https://lucanchurch.com/wp-content/uploads/History_of_the_Baptists_-_Armitage.pdf (pages 192-194)
3. https://www.placefortruth.org/blog/claudius-turin-%E2%80%93-iconoclast-bishop
4. https://www.bl.uk/anglo-saxons/articles/religion-in-anglo-saxon-kingdoms#:~:text=Pope%20Gregory%20I%20(590%E2%80%93604,the%20Anglo%2DSaxons%20to%20Christianity.
5. https://www.britannica.com/topic/Church-of-England
6. https://en.wikipedia.org/wiki/Bible_translations
7. https://www.britannica.com/topic/limbo-Roman-Catholic-theology
8. https://www.westminster-abbey.org/about-the-abbey/history/benedictine-monastery
9. https://www.britannica.com/topic/publishing/The-medieval-book
10. https://www.historydefined.net/what-was-a-priests-role-during-the-middle-ages/
11. https://www.historyextra.com/period/medieval/monks-sex-drink-gamble-history-pope/
12. https://www.newadvent.org/cathen/08426b.htm
13. https://www.newadvent.org/cathen/02429a.htm

About Kharis Publishing

Kharis Publishing, an imprint of Kharis Media LLC, is a leading Christian and inspirational book publisher based in Aurora, Chicago metropolitan area, Illinois. Kharis' dual mission is to give voice to under-represented writers (including women and first-time authors) and equip orphans in developing countries with literacy tools. That is why, for each book sold, the publisher channels some of the proceeds into providing books and computers for orphanages in developing countries so that these kids may learn to read, dream, and grow. For a limited time, Kharis Publishing is accepting unsolicited queries for nonfiction (Christian, self-help, memoirs, business, health, and wellness) from qualified leaders, professionals, pastors, and ministers. Learn more at: About Us - Kharis Publishing - Accepting Manuscript